CONSUMED

Keegan's Chronicles Book One

JULIA CRANE

Consumed: Keegan's Chronicles
Copyright © 2011 by Julia Crane
Published by Valknut Press
All rights reserved.
ISBN-13: 9780983752028

Edited by Claire Teter
Cover art by Eden Crane Designs
Book formatting by CyberWitch Press

For my daughter

Chapter 1

Keegan rushed for the door. Stopping briefly in the doorway, she turned to stare at Rourk with slight smile playing across her face. Her chosen was beautiful. The sun gleaming through the open windows reflected off his soft, rust colored hair. His cool grey eyes met hers and her heart raced. It took every ounce of her self-control not to return to his arms.

Donald deserved more than that. She had to find him.

"Keegan, don't." Rourk's voice was filled with pain. He took a single step forward, his khaki pants rustling in the dead silence of the room. Keegan gazed a moment longer, taking in his messy hair, his plain black t-shirt—everything that made him Rourk.

"I'll be back. I promise." She tore her eyes from him and she was gone.

It was cool outside. Fall had arrived early for Tennessee; it was usually still hot for Keegan's birthday. She pulled the long sleeves of her sweater over her hands, shivering. It was still warmer than Alaska.

Keegan glanced around in the hope of seeing Donald, but he was in his tiger form so he was probably long gone. Her family's property was huge—he had so many places to hide. The woods spread around her, dim and thick even under the bright afternoon sunshine. He could be anywhere.

Frustration and confusion rushed through her body. She wanted to talk to Donald, but she also longed to be inside with Rourk.

She had never expected her bond with Rourk to come back or to hurt Donald, the shy and sweet shape shifter she'd had started to fall for over the past year. The Great Battle —being killed and brought back to life with black magic— severed her bond to Rourk. Afterwards, she couldn't even remember meeting Rourk, let alone their time together. She'd broken one good man's heart, and now, with the bond restored, she was about to break the heart of another.

Suddenly, everything had changed again. She groaned, ran her hands through her tangled mess of auburn hair, and headed towards the woods.

After an hour of walking, she knew it was useless. She couldn't really blame Donald for disappearing; if she had been in his position, she probably would too. Sitting down on the enormous trunk of a fallen tree, she sighed and looked around, rubbing at the goosebumps on her skin. The leaves were turning vibrant shades of red, orange, and yellow, and were just starting to fall off the trees. She grabbed a leaf from the ground at her feet and spun it around between her fingers.

It was hard for her to believe a year ago today on her seventeenth birthday her life path had changed so dramatically.

Suddenly, she felt fur rub up against her arm. *How had he snuck up on her?* She turned and rubbed his head with both hands, giving him a sad smile.

"Turn back into your human form so we can talk," Keegan pleaded.

The tiger shook its head, his feet shuffling among the leaves as he circled her.

"Fine." She closed her eyes, letting her hands rest in her lap. "I'm so sorry. I really never dreamed this would happen. You know an elf's bond to their chosen is too strong to fight. I've never heard of an elf that was able to resist their chosen. My aunt Brigid tried for a while, but even she gave in."

The tiger lay down at her feet, warming them. She opened her eyes. His big blue eyes were sparkling and a tear ran down his face. She moved to wipe it away, but he jerked his head back.

"I could lie to you and tell you that we can try," she told him quietly. "I think we both know it would not work. It would just be prolonging the inevitable. Donald, you are very special to me and always will be. This last year that I spent with you gave me some of the happiest times of my life." Keegan leaned to run her hand through the soft fur of the tiger's back. "I will never forget the time we've had together. I just don't think it's fair of me to lead you on. I think we need to accept that our time is over."

The tiger laid his head between his paws and moaned as if he were in pain, avoiding her eyes.

"Please, talk to me."

The tiger rose up to his full form and walked around her body, nudging her as he went. His fur felt so soft and warm against her skin. Keegan wrapped her arms around the big cat's neck and pulled him close to her. It sounded as if he were purring.

"I'm sorry." Keegan wiped her tears with one hand, still clinging to him.

The tiger pulled away. He let out a loud roar that echoed through the trees and sprinted off, his powerful body moving so fast he was gone before she knew it. Keegan's heart ached at the thought of causing such pain to someone she cared for. She hoped someday he would be able to forgive her.

Once he was out of sight, she slowly made her way back to the house. She wasn't sure she was ready to face Rourk. Although, just thinking of him made her pulse race and her face flush. As much as she cared about Donald, he had never had this affect on her. As she reached the door, her stomach was in knots. She took a deep breath before she pushed the heavy wooden door open.

Thaddeus and Rourk were sitting in the living room when she walked in. Rourk's brow was furrowed, his hands gripped his thighs. She met his gaze, and saw his concern melt into relief. He let out a deep sigh, and his body visibly relaxed.

Thaddeus stood up, tugged his hooded sweatshirt down over his blue jeans from where it had bunched against the couch. "I'm going to play

Xbox. I'll see you later, Rourk."

"Not so fast." Keegan glared at him, her hands planted on her hips. She wanted to scream at him for keeping his secrets so well, but she tried to calm herself instead. It wouldn't be nice to freeze him accidentally. "Why didn't you tell me about all of this? You could have at least given me a warning, or heaven forbid, a choice."

"You *could* tell me thank you." Thaddeus raised an eyebrow and gave her one of his famous impish grins.

"You crushed Donald." Keegan wrapped her arms around herself and looked down at her feet, trying to erase the memory of the tiger's sad eyes.

"Donald will be fine." His tone was matter-of-fact.

"How can you be so sure? Did you have a vision?" Keegan looked up, her eyes wide.

"Let's just say there's a white tiger in his future. I know it's hard for you to believe Keegan, but he will get over you," Thaddeus said sarcastically, and with that, he turned and headed up the stairs.

Keegan was surprised to feel both relief and a pang of jealousy at the thought of Donald loving someone else. She glanced over at Rourk, who had been staring at her silently during the exchange.

"I still don't think this is fair." Keegan pouted, folding her arms across her chest. *And I want to know what you're thinking, Rourk. Can you still love me?*

As if hearing her unspoken question, Rourk stood up and crossed the room until he was in front of her. He was bigger than she recalled, and the softness of youth in his features had been replaced by the harsher angles of manhood. It had been almost a year since the last time she saw him. She stared up at his rugged face, thrilled and apprehensive to realize he was there to claim her. Everything about him was intense; his gaze, his muscular body, the tension and energy between them. She looked up into his eyes and knew she would follow him anywhere. The moment he touched her, she allowed her body to melt into his.

He really is mine, this time, forever.

"I've waited so long for this day." His voice sounded rough. He rested his chin on her head and pulled her closer, his strong arms cradling her waist in a way that made her feel special, cherished. It was futile to resist their connection, and she wondered how strong black magic was to counter what she felt in her mate's arms. She'd been an oblivious fool, but no more.

As of now, their fates were sealed. They belonged to each other.

Chapter 2

Keegan's mother came through the door with her hands filled with groceries. Her pale cheeks were flushed from the chill outside and her ginger, pixie-style hair was windblown. She stopped mid-step and grinned, balancing the largest of the bags on her hip. "Well, hello Rourk. I hope you are staying for dinner?"

"If it's ok with Keegan. I would love to stay for dinner. Here let me help you." He stood from the couch in one smooth movement and crossed the living room. Taking the bags from her mom, he headed towards the kitchen.

Keegan's mom waited until he was out of earshot, her eyes lit with excitement, and then said, "Keegan! Does this mean what I think it means?"

Face serious, Keegan met her mother's blue eyes. "Yes, the bond is back. I'm sure you're happy."

"You are not happy about this?"

"I don't know, Mom. It's all so sudden. I just broke Donald's heart. I barely know Rourk, but I'm so drawn to him I can't do anything *but* be with him."

Keegan turned to watch Rourk with a small smile. Beyond the counter that separated living room from kitchen, he was bustling around as if he had been doing it forever. He was putting her mother's groceries away. Keegan sighed. "I guess I am a little happy. He's perfect isn't he?"

"Yes, he is your perfect match." Her mother nodded, and a big grin broke across her face. "This is so exciting. We need to start making plans."

Startled, Keegan asked, "Plans for what?"

"Your wedding, of course. There is so much to do. I haven't given it any thought since you lost the bond. Do you want the hand fasting to take place on the property or somewhere else? Ohh...we could have the wedding in Ireland. Keegan, we are going to have so much fun shopping for a dress." Her mother's enthusiasm was infectious, but the whole idea was crazy.

"My wedding? I barely know him. I just started college. There is no way I am getting married right now." Planting her hand on her hip, she glared at her mother.

Emerald rolled her eyes. "Keegan, you know that is the elfin tradition. You meet your mate at eighteen and you get married. Tradition is the foundation of our society. I married your father a month after we met. It's the way it is. This is not news to you, so stop overreacting."

Shaking her head vehemently, Keegan stood firm. "You can forget it. It's not happening. At least not until I finish college. I'm sure Rourk will understand."

"Understand what?" Rourk appeared at Keegan's side and looked back and forth between the two women, his brow furrowed.

Turning her glare from her mother to her chosen, Keegan said, "My mom wants to start planning our wedding. I told her I'm not getting married until I graduate college."

Rourk grinned, shoving his hands in his pockets. "You are so cute when you are angry."

"Are you ok with waiting?" Keegan asked, exasperated.

"I think this is something we can talk about later. I don't see the need to rush into anything." Rourk put his arm around Keegan and looked down at her with a big smile. "I'm just happy our bond has been returned."

Keegan shot her mother a satisfied look and said, "I told you so."

Her mother rolled her eyes and headed for the kitchen. "Well, we'll see what your father says about this."

Keegan smiled at Rourk after her mother was gone. "Thank you, for understanding. We have our whole lives ahead of us. I don't think we need to rush into getting married."

Rourk reached over and touched the side of her face, his eyes searching. "Whatever you want is fine with me. As far as I am concerned, we are bonded and that is enough."

"Are you sure?" Keegan touched the side of his arm and electricity shot through her. She jumped. "Did you feel that?"

Rourk laughed. "Yes, Keegan, it always feels

like that when we touch."

She grinned. "That is pretty cool. I still don't recall our time before the bond broke. I wish I did."

He wrapped his arms around her and gave her a brief but tight hug. "We will start fresh today. So how is school going? I have no idea what you have been doing this last year. It was torture for me not to be able to see you through my mind's eye."

"Can you see me now?"

Rourk closed his eyes and thought of Keegan. She materialized as clear as if he was looking at her in front of him. He opened his eyes and grinned. "I can see you again. Every night I would close my eyes and think of you and all I could see was darkness."

"I'm sorry." Keegan stared down at her hands.

"It's not your fault. You have nothing to be sorry about. Tell me about school."

Shrugging, Keegan sighed. "It's ok. It's actually a lot harder than I expected. I've always been used to not having to study. Now I actually have to pay attention and take notes. I've made a couple of friends. Really the only thing I enjoy is volunteering at the wildlife station, and taking photos. It's so beautiful there. You have to come see it."

"I would love to come see you. I get weekends off most of the time now that we are in the advanced training. They don't treat us like children any longer."

"What about you? How's your training going? My father told me you were making quite the impression." Keegan tugged him to the couch and pulled him down beside her.

"It's going well. I'm going to be stationed in Washington. It was the closest I could get to Alaska."

Keegan's hand covered her mouth. She stared at him wide-eyed. "You were trying to get stationed closer to me? Even though our bond was gone?"

"The bond was gone for you," he said quietly, gently squeezing her hands between his. "For me it was as strong as ever. I've always wanted to be close to you."

"Why did you leave then? You could have tried harder." She couldn't help the tiny bit of irritation in her voice.

"Keegan, leaving you was the hardest thing I've ever had to do in my life. I left because it wasn't fair for me to stay here. You were too young and besides I saw you with the shapeshifter in the woods." Rourk clenched his jaw.

Keegan froze, her heart pounding. "You saw us? Why didn't you say anything?"

"I was too hurt. I had to get away before I did something stupid. I knew you weren't doing anything wrong. You had not yet turned eighteen. You were *supposed* to be dating until you met me. Things just got messed up with the black magic." Rourk paused briefly. "Hell, I couldn't even blame the shapeshifter. Why wouldn't he be attracted to you?"

"I'm glad you came back for me." Keegan reached over with both hands and pulled his head towards hers. She wrapped her arms around his neck, and pressed her lips against his. The electricity raced through her body.

Rourk pulled away and looked into her eyes. "I love you."

Keegan sighed and snuggled closer, resting her head on his shoulder. "I love you too. I don't think I can ever recall feeling this content."

The front door opened and her father appeared. A huge grin spread across his face as he caught sight of his daughter. Closing the door firmly, he said, "I see you got quite the birthday present Keegan."

Keegan laughed. "I guess you could say that."

Rourk stood up and shook Richard's hand. They didn't have to say anything, they just exchanged knowing grins.

Emerald came out from the kitchen grinning like a fool. "Isn't this great? I knew it would all work out. Although, your daughter is refusing to get married. She wants to wait until after she graduates college."

Richard shook his head. "Why is it every time Keegan does or says something you don't agree with she is my daughter?" He winked at his wife. "Let's worry about this another day and just enjoy having Rourk back into our family. What's for dinner? I'm starving."

Keegan interrupted whatever her mother was going to say by jumping up and thrusting her hand out for them to see. The ruby was hard to miss with the lights reflecting off it. "I almost forgot to show you my ring." Keegan looked down at her hand, smiling. "I used to dream of this exact ring when I was younger."

"Yes, I recall all the times you asked me what would happen if your chosen didn't give you a ruby ring." Emerald chuckled. "It's beautiful. I love the antique setting and how the ruby is set flush." Emerald glanced over at Rourk. "How long has this been in your family?

Rourk shrugged his shoulders. "I don't know the exact timeframe. My mother passed away when I was too young to understand all of this. I just know it has been many generations."

"Fate is a wonderful thing." Emerald looked over at her husband and they shared a smile.

"Keegan, can't we talk you into a wedding? We're long overdue for a party, and I'm sure the men would love to see Rourk." Her father rubbed his beard, looking at her from thoughtful, hazel eyes.

Keegan shot him a dirty look, then sighed. "Dad, forget it. It's not happening. You'll get your wedding. Just not right away."

Richard looked at Emerald and shrugged. "Don't say I didn't try."

Rourk put his arm around Keegan. "Richard, how is the camp? Have you still been working closely with Creed?"

"Things are going as well as can be expected. Creed has turned out to be a great ally. We're making progress, but as you know it's often one step forward and two back. I don't think we'll be out of a job anytime soon."

Rourk nodded in agreement. "I'm looking forward to getting back to the Army of the Light. I have to admit I have been enjoying the training, and working with the humans. I can understand why it is tradition for elves to join the human army. It's a great experience."

"We look forward to having you back. Did you

sign up for four or six years?"

"Just four. I figured Keegan would be done with college and ready to move back by then. If not, we'll figure something out."

Keegan shivered, leaning into Rourk's side. "I think I'll be ready. Alaska is already freezing and it's only September."

Thaddeus came down the stairs, his heavy footsteps pounding the hardwood. "Rourk, how long are you going to be here?"

Keegan's heart dropped. She hadn't thought he would be leaving soon. They would be separated again. She clung tighter to his waist, peering up at him with her eyes wide.

"I only have a couple of days off. I have to be back by Monday," Rourk told Thaddeus, glancing down at Keegan apologetically.

Keegan pouted, pulling away from his arms. "That's so soon. I have to go back to school on Monday, too. I can't believe we just found each other again and we're already going to be separated."

"You might as well get used to it, Keegan. Rourk is a warrior. He will often be gone," Emerald said matter-of-factly, leaning on the kitchen counter.

"It still doesn't make me happy." Keegan crossed her arms and kicked the floor, her lower lip jutting out even more.

Thaddeus shook his head at Rourk. "I feel bad for you."

They all laughed before going their separate ways to wait on dinner. Her mother ended up making steak for fajitas.

When dinner was ready, they gathered

around the table and chatted. Keegan reached for her second tortilla, and said, "This is good mom. Have you been working on your cooking skills?"

"Keegan, you should know better than to ask that. It's a frozen mix I just had to throw it in the pan and let heat up. Just because elves can't use modern technology in battle doesn't mean we can't use it in the kitchen. Speaking of cooking, I'm surprised you haven't wasted away on your own. Have you been cooking or eating out every meal?"

"A little of both. I've found I actually enjoy cooking but it just kinda sucks cooking for myself."

"You can cook for me next weekend." Rourk grinned at her across the table.

"Really? You will come see me next weekend?" Keegan's face flushed with excitement.

"I will come to see you every chance I get."

Richard pointed his fork and spoke through a mouthful of food. "Don't forget to sign up for frequent flyer programs. You'll have free tickets before you know it."

Emerald rolled her eyes at her husband. "He is obsessed with frequent flyer programs."

Thaddeus took a bite, then asked Rourk, "How's Tommy?"

Rourk grinned. "Tommy is doing great. It's like he's a new man."

"Who's Tommy?" Keegan asked.

"A friend I made during training. He's also going to be stationed in Washington. I can't wait for you to meet him."

"There is so much I don't know about you. For some reason I never pictured you having friends. You sort of come across as a loner." Keegan grabbed her glass and took a sip.

Thaddeus laughed. "I think Tommy is Rourk's first friend."

Keegan frowned, looking intently at her boyfriend. "Is that true?"

"I guess he is. I never really thought about it."

After they finished dinner, Rourk asked, "Would you like to go for a walk?"

She smiled. "Of course!"

Grabbing her phone on the way out the door, she saw she had several texts from her friends asking what had happened after they left.

She slid the phone in her pocket; she would fill them in later.

Chapter 3

Keegan grabbed a sweater before they left the house. She looked at Rourk while she slipped her arms into the green wool. "I get cold easily since I came back from the dead."

"Well, you picked the wrong place to move. You must be freezing in Alaska." Rourk laced his fingers through hers, leading her down the path.

Keegan laughed. "Yeah, it wasn't a very well thought-out plan. I just always wanted to go to Alaska. Their marine biology program is one of the best." She ran her fingers over his hand and giggled. "That is the weirdest thing. I can feel the vibrations from your skin."

He stopped, pulling her near. His hands spanned across her back as he smiled down at her. "I've missed hearing your laugh. Hell, I've missed everything about you."

"Well, looks like you are stuck with me now." Keegan wrapped her arms around his waist, leaning her head against his chest.

"You have always been the only one for me, Keegan." Rourk turned and lightly ran his thumb across her bottom lip before he leaned down to kiss her—softly at first and then with more urgency. He eventually pulled away, his grey eyes searching hers. "I can't lose you again."

"Wow. You keep kissing me like that and you won't have anything to worry about." She nudged him with her hip. Taking hold of Rourk's arm, she pulled him over to a group of large rocks, where she sat down and tugged at him to join her.

"What happened with the shapeshifter?" Rourk leaned down and picked up a small stone, not looking her in the eyes.

"He wouldn't talk to me. I really hurt him, but he's always known this was a possibility." Keegan moved her shoe around on the grass, searching for words. "I told him it was over because I couldn't resist the bond."

"Do you love him?" His eyes met hers and his face was expressionless.

"What?" Keegan looked over at him, surprised by his question. She had asked herself the same thing over and over while she was with Donald.

"I said, do you love him?" Rourk's expression was calm but the edge in his voice gave her no doubt as to how he felt.

Keegan put her hand on his knee and shook her head. "No, I didn't love Donald. I could never bring myself to say the words. I'm not going to lie—I cared about him a lot, and I still do."

"Did you two—you know?" Rourk looked away, staring into the distance. His face was hard.

"Huh? Did we what? Oh… Did we have sex?"

She smiled, touching his face gently. "We didn't have sex. Never even came close to it."

Rourk's entire body relaxed and he let out a barely noticeable sigh.

Keegan wanted to kick the ground. All the pain she had caused Rourk... Curious, she couldn't help but ask. "Would it have mattered if I had been with him in that way?"

"It would tear me apart, but it would not change how I feel about you. I'm glad you were not." Rourk lowered his eyes, one of his hands coming to rest atop hers on his leg.

Keegan gave him a shy smile, scooting closer. "I guess I have been saving myself for you."

"Keegan, I want you to be with me because it's what you want. I don't want you to feel obligated because of the bond." He sounded worried, his statement coming faster than usual.

It broke Keegan's heart that she had hurt him for so long. Now the man she was meant to love—the man she loved—seemed to not think her feelings were real. *What do I say to make this right?*

"We're elves, Rourk. This is what we do. I've dreamed of meeting my chosen since I was a little girl. We got sidetracked, that's all. I believe we are exactly where we are meant to be." Keegan looked up at the sky and spread her arms wide. "Someone up there believes we are meant to be. Who am I to argue with fate? I'm not going anywhere. I want to learn everything about you, and spend as much time with you as I can." Hoping she had said the right thing to prove her love, she rested her head back on his shoulder.

"I'm so glad you said that, Keegan." Rourk closed his eyes briefly, one arm slipping around her shoulders so he could hold her tight. "I have been worried you were angry the bond was back. I thought maybe you were wishing it could be changed."

Laughing, Keegan said, "If I were angry the ground would be frozen. I'm not angry. I was just caught by surprise."

He pushed her away so he could look at her, one hand brushing her hair back. "Thaddeus told me about the frozen issue. He also said that Donald was able to help you control it. What if I don't have that same affect on you?"

Keegan thought it was cute that he had focused on *that* part of the freezing. "I've gotten better at controlling my temper. I've been using my father's breathing exercises and my mom gives me distant healings, which help keep me calmer." She paused. "It's too bad that issue didn't go away when the bond came back. I guess that would be asking for too much."

"It could be a good tool to have."

"Always thinking like a soldier..." Keegan teased.

"It's what I am."

Keegan jumped up, putting both her hands on his shoulders. He was so gorgeous when he looked surprised. "I just realized something. You are going to be in Washington and that's where Anna goes to school— in Seattle. Maybe I can transfer there next semester." Excitement lit up her face and her cheeks flushed. "I'm going to have to start researching the schools."

"You would do that?"

"Of course. Don't tell my parents, but I really don't care for Alaska. I mean it's beautiful and all, but the malls close early, and I don't have any real friends."

Rourk's grin was wry. "Your secret is safe with me."

Keegan plopped back down on the rock. "Ouch." She rubbed the side of her leg. "I can't believe we have to be separated soon. When will you move to Washington?"

Rourk pulled her towards him. "It depends. Two to four months. Definitely by the beginning of the new year. I will come see you every weekend unless training prohibits it. Plus, I'll have time off for the holidays."

That made her remember her Christmas present. "Speaking of holidays, I never told you thank you for the lens. I've been keeping a scrap book for you of photos I've taken."

"Really? I can't wait to see it."

"Well, you will have to wait. It's at my apartment in Alaska."

"How do you like having your own place?"

"I hate it. It's so quiet. I need to get a dog." Keegan grinned. "I always pictured us having an English bulldog named Santa."

Rourk laughed loudly. "That's pretty funny. I say next weekend we go in search of a bulldog."

Keegan threw her arms around him and squeezed him. "We're going to have so much fun together."

Rourk stood up and pulled her with him. "It's getting late. I should probably head home."

Keegan pouted. "I don't want you to leave. Maybe you can stay the night."

He lifted an eyebrow. "I don't think that would be appropriate."

"Well, then let's just stay up all night out here."

"Are you sure? Your parents might get upset."

"Are you kidding me? They are so excited our bond is back, I don't think they would care what we did. Plus, I'm eighteen now." She smiled sweetly.

"Ok, let me call my father and let him know I won't be home tonight." Rourk pulled his phone out of his pocket and flipped it open, walking away as he made his call.

Keegan watched him, thinking it was adorable he still had an old school phone. He probably didn't even have a laptop. She would have to bring him into the technology world.

Rourk strode back towards her. She loved his confident walk. "You were right. He was thrilled to hear the bond was back and happy to hear we are staying together tonight."

"I told ya. So, what do you want to do?" Keegan rocked back and forth on her heels.

"I don't care as long as I am with you. We can sit here all night, or go for a drive. What time is it anyway?"

Keegan looked down at her phone. "It's almost midnight. We could always go to an all-night diner and have some coffee."

"That sounds great. Should you run in and tell your parents?"

"Nah, they are probably asleep. I'll send my mom a text though, just in case."

They walked back down the path to the house and towards Rourk's truck. When Keegan saw the tiger sitting in the middle of the driveway, her heart ached for Donald. Rourk must have felt her tense, because he turned and saw the shapeshifter, too.

Rourk kept his eyes on the feline while he opened the door, and Keegan slid into the truck. The tiger walked closer and Keegan's heart raced as she thought, *Is he going to attack Rourk?* She watched as the two of them stared at each other. Finally, the tiger turned and slowly stalked away.

Once Rourk was in the truck, Keegan turned towards him. "I'm sorry I've made such a mess of things."

"I told you, it's not your fault. Hopefully, the shapeshifter is smart enough to realize there is nothing he can do to change things. As much as I hate the thought of him being around you, I know what it feels like to lose you, and I feel somewhat bad for him."

Keegan sighed, letting her head fall back to the headrest. "Thank you for being so understanding. I'm sure this has all been hard for you."

Rourk glanced over at her, and then back to the road as he put the car into gear and aimed for the road. "You have no idea. I'm just glad it's behind us and we can move forward."

Keegan slid over in the middle so she could be closer to him. She placed her hand on his thigh and laid her head against him. "Did it feel this natural when we met the first time?"

"Yes." His lips brushed her hair. "It felt as if we had known each other our whole lives in an instant. The memories of the time we spent together were the only things that kept me going."

"You will have to tell me all about our time

together. I have the photographs, I just don't have the story behind them." Keegan wanted to remember more than *anything*, but no matter how hard she tried, it was impossible. It made her want to cry that she had lost those memories of him.

"Another day," Rourk answered quietly. "Today, I want to enjoy the present and not worry about the past."

"Ok. Why don't you tell me about your training?" Keegan sat up so she could watch him in the dim cabin. Every so often a car would pass and the headlights would illuminate his face.

"There's not much to tell. It's not that much different from the elfin military training. It gets frustrating sometimes because I know better ways to do things, but I can't let on. I'm in the weapons training. It's pretty amazing how advanced some of the weapons are."

Keegan laughed. "I was just thinking when I saw you with your old school flip phone that you weren't very technologically inclined. Do you even have a laptop?"

"Should I?

"Ah yeah, how else am I going to talk to you when we are separated? Put that on our list of things to do when you come visit. Actually, we'll do that tomorrow. So you can have it for Monday. Do you have your own room?"

"Yeah, we have our own rooms now. They are pretty small but they work. It's nice to have the privacy."

"I probably can't come visit you, can I?"

Rourk thought about it for a minute. "I think it's best if you wait until I get to Fort Lewis, in

Washington. I don't like the idea of you coming into the barracks. I should be able to get my own place there. I'll probably have Tommy as a roommate. "

Keegan shrugged. "Ok, as long as you come visit me."

"Every chance I get. You will probably get sick of me."

"Somehow I doubt that."

Rourk pulled into the diner and parked. They strolled inside, their arms wrapped around each other.

After they were settled with menus and drinks, Keegan stared at Rourk across the table. "How did this happen so quickly? I went from not knowing anything about you to feeling like we have been together forever."

"I think we can thank your brother." Rourk's half-smile made her heart skip a beat.

"Yeah, I was probably a little too harsh with him." Keegan looked down at her ring and back up at Rourk with a look of pure adoration. "A magical ring."

They stayed up for hours talking and driving before ending up in the woods, where they watched the sun rise. Rourk dropped her off as the sun had finally crested over the horizon and the birds were singing their morning songs.

Keegan stood in the front doorway, watching his truck pull away and felt a deep sadness wash over her. She felt like chasing after the truck and jumping in.

Chapter 4

When Keegan walked through the door, she found her mother at the kitchen table reading a book.

Her mom laid the book face down and looked up. "I take it you had a good night?" she said, then took a sip of tea.

Keegan sat down across from her mom and rested her chin in her hands with a sigh. "It was wonderful. Do you always feel like this around Dad?"

Her mother smiled. "Of course. It's the way it works."

"Do you guys feel electricity when you touch?" Keegan slumped back in the chair, a wistful smile on her face.

"Yes. Not that your father doesn't drive me crazy at times, but overall I feel happiest when he is around."

"So the electricity thing doesn't go away with time?" Keegan raised an eyebrow.

"No, but you do get used to it though. Once it

becomes normal, you don't notice it till you're separated and he returns."

Keegan stood up and rubbed her stomach, grimacing. "I'm going to grab something to eat. My stomach feels a little funny."

Walking over to the bread box, Keegan opened it and pulled out the loaf. She dropped a couple of slices into the toaster. When it was ready, Keegan buttered it and topped it with some cinnamon.

"Where's Thad?" she asked.

"In his room, as usual," her mother answered, flipping her book over and turning the page.

"Ok, I'm going to go talk to him." Keegan chomped on the toast as she mounted the stairs. She couldn't stop smiling, thinking about her time with Rourk.

Just before her hand hit the door to knock, her brother yelled, "Come in."

"Even after all these years it's still freaky when you do that." Keegan opened the door and glanced around at his nearly empty room.

It always looked strange to her that Thaddeus only had a bed and a dresser. It was never really messy in his room, either. Between the stark white walls and the blah carpet, it looked like a hotel room instead of that of a teenage boy.

Everybody likes different stuff, I guess, Keegan told herself. She walked over and sat on Thaddeus's bed to watch as he killed zombies on the Xbox.

She let him blow some stuff up first before she finally spoke. "Thanks for bringing back the bond. I'm sorry I acted like a jerk earlier."

"It wasn't really me. Anna did most of the work." He didn't bother to turn around. His fingers were flying over the controller buttons.

"Really?" Keegan said, surprised. She stared at his head full of short, auburn hair. "Well, I guess I need to thank her."

"Probably a good idea." Thaddeus paused. Keegan wasn't sure if it was for effect or because he couldn't speak for too long of a period and play at the same time. He went on. "She thinks you are mad at her."

"Ugh. I forgot to text her back." Keegan searched for her phone in her pockets, but it wasn't there. *Must have left it downstairs.* "I lost track of time with Rourk. I still can't believe he is my chosen. He's everything and more of what I used to dream as a little girl."

"He's a good guy. You better not mess up your chance with him." Gunshots rang from the television and more zombies fell.

"I won't." She stood up to leave, and swayed. She reached out with one hand to grab the bed post and steady herself. Her head felt so light. "I'm going to go lay down for a bit. I'm not feeling so hot."

Thaddeus took one hand off the controller and waved it in her direction. His eyes were still glued to the TV. "Shut the door on your way out."

"Yeah, yeah. We all know you like your privacy. You really should get out more."

For the first time since she came in the room, Thaddeus actually looked up at her. Granted, it was a glare and it lasted two seconds before he went back to his game, but it was acknowledgment.

Keegan giggled. Some things never changed. She had to admit, she did miss having her little brother around.

Speaking of little brothers... Keegan thought, frowning. She had barely seen Warrick since she had been home. After her nap, she'd have to go find him.

She closed Thaddeus's bedroom door and walked down the hall to her own room. Her head was pounding. *I'm probably just tired from staying up all night.* And there was the time difference from Alaska, too.

Keegan walked in her bedroom and looked around. She smiled. Her sweater was still on the back of the chair, and her brush was on the floor. Her mother had left everything exactly as it was the day she left.

She missed being home. College was cool and all, but she was lonely in Alaska. At least Rourk would be coming to see her; that brought a smile to her face.

She was exhausted from staying up all night. She peeled off her clothes and crawled into bed, dozing off quickly.

Next thing she knew she woke up to a sharp pain in her chest and a horrible pain in her stomach. She felt like she was having a panic attack—or what she imagined must be what a panic attack.

Keegan picked up her phone and texted her mom. *Can you come here?*

She curled into a ball beneath the covers and took a few deep breaths, trying to get past the pain. A couple minutes later there was a light knock at the door before it opened.

Her mom came through—a shadow in the pale hall light as it spilled into the dark room. "Keegan? What's wrong?"

Keegan felt a little better having her mom near. "I think I need a healing. My chest and stomach hurts. Maybe I ate something bad."

Her mother walked up to her bed and sat down, the bed springs squeaking. She touched her hand lightly to Keegan's head. "It wasn't something you ate. It's the bond."

Her mother's hand was cool and comforting. Keegan's eyes widened and she clutched the pillow beneath her cheek. "What do you mean 'the bond'?"

Her mom gave her a wry smile, barely visible in the dim room. "Like everything in life, there are consequences to having a magical bond. It cannot be perfect. Rarely can you get pleasure without pain." She shifted on the bed. "When you are separated from your chosen, you are going to experience physical pain until you are reunited."

"What? Why didn't anyone ever tell me this?" Keegan pulled the blankets up to her chin with a grimace. *I'll have to deal with this often?*

"And ruin the excitement of meeting your chosen?" Emerald ran a hand through her short hair. She stared at Keegan, her brow furrowed. "There usually has to be great distance between you to cause this much discomfort. Rourk doesn't live that far away."

"You're telling me that if Rourk came back the pain would go away?" Keegan eyed at her mother skeptically.

"Yes. The closer he gets, the more the pain lessens." She brushed Keegan's hair back, her eyes shiny in the dark. "I always know your father is on his way home long before he arrives."

"Dad is gone so much! I've never noticed you to be in pain."

"I am a healer, Keegan. My body heals itself, although it cannot heal the heart. So, my heart aches—much like yours is now—until your father comes back."

"Well, that's just lovely," Keegan said sarcastically. She pulled the covers higher with a *humph.* "Is Rourk in pain now?"

"Yes, Keegan." She pursed her lips. "You may not have realized, but Rourk was in pain the whole time you were separated."

Keegan's heart skipped a beat and a flood of anger filled her. She hated that she had caused him physical pain. "Why didn't I feel pain before?"

"He was always close by before your bond broke. If you recall, you went into that slump once you couldn't see him again."

"I can't believe he's been in physical pain since he left to join the military."

"Your father is glad for the pain. He says it makes him never forget me. Rourk probably feels the same way." Her mother's eyes softened. "He loves you, Keegan."

Keegan was silent as she processed all the information her mother had given her.

Her mom put a gentle hand to Keegan's face. "Do you want me to give you a healing?"

"No. I'm going to call him. To see if he will come back. I want him to tell me that what you say is true. "

Her mother laughed. "You always have to see things to believe them. Call him."

Keegan made the call and within minutes, the pain had subsided. She waited impatiently in the kitchen with her mother, pretending to drink hot chocolate. Her heart fluttered when she heard the knock from the front hall.

Keegan hurried to let him in. She flung the door open and wrapped her arms around him. "I'm so glad you came. Were you in pain?"

Rourk pulled back and looked down at her. "You were in pain?"

"You weren't?"

Rourk's hair was tousled as if he'd just rolled out of bed. He was wearing the same pair of pants and shirt as he'd worn the night before.

Keegan thought he looked beautiful. But then she felt guilty for pulling him out of bed and all the way to her house in the country after neither one of them had gotten much sleep. *I'm so selfish*, she thought.

"Not really pain," Rourk answered, cupping her face in his hands. "There was a slight discomfort, but nothing like when I am far away from you." Rourk glanced over at Emerald.

She met his eyes but said nothing.

"How much pain on a level from 1-10?" Rourk demanded, his eyes on Keegan's.

"I don't know. Maybe a 6? I'm not good at measuring pain."

Rourk wrapped his arms around Keegan and pulled her to him before saying, "Emerald, is that normal?"

Her mother shrugged. "No, Rourk. Not as far as I know. However, since my healing energies heal me, I never feel the full affect. Maybe we should call Katrina or Brigid. They would know better."

Rourk nodded. "Please."

Emerald grabbed her phone from the table and dialed. She smiled at Rourk when Katrina answered. "Hey sis, I have a question for you. When Drew is gone, how far away does he have to be in order for you to feel the pain of his absence?"

Her sister was silent for a moment on the other end of the line. "Well, that's an odd question. Hmm, I would say at least four hours away."

"Four hours!?" Emerald closed her eyes. "Ok, thanks, was just wondering. I'll explain more later, but suffice it to say that Keegan and Rourk got their bond back."

Emerald pulled the phone from her ear and they could all hear Kat's "Woohoo."

"I swear Kat, you are just as bad as a teenager. I'll call you later." Emerald hung up the phone and turned to face them.

"So, this is not typical. Keegan you always have to be the exception don't you?" Her mother took a deep breath and looked at Rourk.

Keegan pulled away from Rourk's embrace and crossed her arms. "Hey, I didn't even know *anything* about any of this till I woke up tonight with the worst pain ever."

"We're not blaming you, Keegan," her mother said. "I'm worried this might have something to do with the black magic."

"Maybe our bond is just stronger than most." Keegan smiled at Rourk.

Emerald shook her head. "I've never heard of anyone's bond being stronger than others. Elfin bonds should be equal across the board. You have been around enough elfin families to know that."

"Well, you did say I was exceptional." Keegan smirked.

"I would have to agree with that statement." Rourk rubbed the back of her neck. His calloused fingers sent chills down her spine.

"Focus you two. This is serious. Soon you will be separated several thousand miles. What if the pain gets worse with distance?" Emerald paced back and forth deep in thought.

Rourk dropped his hand and sat down in one of the chairs. With his elbows on the table, he let his head drop into his hands. "I can't stand the thought of Keegan being in pain because of me."

Keegan walked over and put her hand on his shoulder. "I'm sure it won't be that bad. It's worth it to be with you."

Rourk looked up surprised. "Do you mean that?"

"Of course I do." She turned her back to him and plopped down on his lap, wrapping her arms around his neck.

Rourk buried his head in her shoulder. "I'm so sorry, Keegan. The last thing I wanted to do was cause you pain."

"We won't even know how bad it is until I get to Alaska. Where are you stationed right now anyway? I guess I should have asked that earlier." *I can really be an airhead*, she thought with an inward chuckle.

"Fort Bragg, North Carolina. A long way away from where you are."

"Well, soon you will be in Washington, and that is much closer. I need to start looking into transferring schools."

Her mother glanced up, eyes wide. "I think that is a great idea! Why don't I come back to Alaska with you so I can be there if you need a healing. I can do the distance healings, but they are not as effective. Maybe your brother can figure something out with magic to help lessen the pain."

"That sounds great, Mom." Keegan didn't want to admit it to herself, but the thought of having her mom in Alaska made her happy. She'd been so lonely and bored living so far away.

"I need to go work on some healing remedies. I'll see you guys later, ok?"

"Thank you," Rourk told her with a grin.

Emerald just smiled and disappeared through the doorway.

Chapter 5

Keegan turned her attention back to Rourk.

"What do you want to do today? I know one thing for sure. I am not leaving your side until I have to board the plane." Rourk squeezed her hand and looked away.

But Keegan saw the distress on his face. It was obvious that it *killed* him he was causing her pain. And they both knew there would be more to come.

"I don't really care. We could just hang out together. If you want, we can go on an actual date." Keegan ran her hand up the side of his arm, unable to resist touching him. "I think that would be fun. We have so much to learn about each other."

His face lit up. "I would love to go on a date with you. Do you have anything special in mind?"

Keegan thought for a moment. "There's a new movie out I've been wanting to see. We could do a repeat of our first date." She gave him a sly smile.

"I think it will end much better this time."

"Pizza and a movie sounds good." He gently kissed her forehead.

Keegan yawned. "I didn't get much sleep. I'm still tired. Let's go in the living room so I can lie down."

Rourk sat in the corner of the couch so that Keegan could stretch out with her head on his thigh. He ran his hands through her hair, staring at her face as her eyes fluttered shut. She was sleeping in a matter of minutes.

Rourk thought about how lucky he was. He leaned his head back against the couch and worried about being separated from her again. A sharp pain pierced his heart. He almost wished he hadn't signed up for the human military. But, he made a commitment, so he brushed the thought aside. He and Keegan would figure something out. They had to...

Keegan stirred. Her cheek was numb from Rourk's leg. *How long was I asleep?*

She rolled over and looked up at him. He was rubbing his eyes. "Did you fall asleep too?" she asked, giving him a sleepy smile.

Rourk nodded. "How are you feeling?"

"Much better after a nap." She stretched out her legs and wiggled her toes. "I'm hungry."

"Aren't you always?"

"Hey!" She swatted his arm. "Yeah, I guess I am always hungry. I like to eat. What can I say?"

Keegan rolled to a sitting position and stretched. She stood and offered her hands to Rourk, pulling him to his feet. They moved into the kitchen.

"I can make you something to eat if you want." Rourk stood behind the grey granite counter. She noticed it matched his eyes.

"Are you sure? You know how to cook?" She was skeptical.

"Yes." He laughed. "I know how to cook. I cooked for you at the cabin. I know you don't recall—I made you vegetarian meals."

"Umm, Ok, sure. You really seem too good to be true." Keegan smiled at him and waved towards the kitchen. "It's all yours."

"Your mom won't mind?"

"My mom spends as little time as possible in the kitchen. She won't care, I promise."

Rourk walked over and peered into the fridge. "Your mom keeps the fridge stocked."

"Well, we are a house full of elves with big appetites."

Keegan watched as he took out some vegetables. He washed and chopped the celery and carrots expertly, then grabbed the ranch dressing out of the fridge and placed it before her. "Here. Snack on this while I cook something up."

She picked up a piece of celery and dipped it, then smiled. "I guess I'll keep you around."

Rourk walked around the counter to where she sat on the stool. "I sure hope so because I can't lose you again."

Keegan bit her lip and looked up, her eyes sparkling. "I'm not going anywhere."

Rourk leaned down and kissed her. One of the amazing slow and passionate kisses she'd come to expect from him.

"You must have driven the girls crazy," she

murmured as he pulled away.

Rourk shook his head. "It's so odd you don't recall our time together. Keegan, you are my first and only girlfriend."

"What? Are you serious? You're so hot. I don't believe it." Though, if she was going to be honest, she loved the thought of being the only one for him. The thought of anyone else having ever kissed him made her the tiniest bit jealous.

"I've never been interested in anyone but you. Although, if Tommy had his way I would be dating half the state." Rourk chuckled and went back to cooking.

"Oh really—I can't wait to meet this Tommy character." She narrowed her eyes, pointing her half-eaten celery stick at Rourk as menacingly as she could.

"Character is a good word for him. You'll like him."

Rourk pulled out chicken and cut it into strips as the pan was heating up. Keegan found that she loved watching him cook. He looked so at ease in the kitchen, which was odd because he screamed soldier when you saw him in public. She really couldn't wait to find out more about him.

She smiled to herself. *We have a lifetime ahead of us to do so.*

"What time is your plane leaving?" Keegan asked, crunching into another celery stick.

He didn't turn to look at her, but his voice was subdued. "Tomorrow at 9 pm. It was the latest flight out I could get."

Keegan shifted uncomfortably on the stool. "I'm leaving at 6pm. I have a long flight. And classes Monday morning."

He was silent a moment. "This is going to be hard."

"I know," Keegan said. She sighed. "I've never felt this way before. I feel panicked at the thought of being separated from you."

Rourk looked down at the pan and moved the chicken around. "I know. I'm not looking forward to leaving you. I just got you back. It's going to kill me to see you get on the plane."

Keegan realized she was choked up, and didn't answer. Instead, she covered a carrot in dressing and ate it.

Rourk scooped up the chicken and placed it on a bed of lettuce and tomatoes then sprinkled some shredded cheese on top. He placed it in front of her along with the dressing. "I hope this is good enough."

Keegan gave him a look of adoration. "It's perfect. Go get yours so we can eat."

They ate in silence, neither wanting to talk about the fact that they would be saying goodbye soon. Keegan felt anxious anytime she thought about him leaving her. *Please let it not be as bad as I think it will,* she thought.

After they ate, Keegan said, "I'm going to jump in the shower, then we can go shopping for your laptop."

Rourk grabbed her hand and pulled her towards him. "I'll be right here when you get back." His kiss sent fire through her body.

She smiled, then turned on her heel and ran up the stairs. Her cell phone was laying on her desk. She grabbed it and sent Anna a text. *Thank you!*

You're welcome. Everything is good?

Perfect other than we have to be separated tomorrow.

Yeah, that sucks.

Guess who is moving to Washington next semester.

NO WAY! We should be roommates.

That would be crazy!

Ok I have to jump in the shower. I'll talk to you once I get back in Alaska.

Bye.

Keegan held the phone tight to her chest with a huge grin across her face. She jumped in the shower and got dressed in record time. *I'm glad I left so many of my clothes here instead of taking them all to Alaska,* she thought as she shimmied into a pair of faded jeans. She pulled on a pale blue sweater, and then quickly applied some mascara and blush. One last look in the mirror, and she ran back downstairs to Rourk.

He was sitting on the couch with her father. He jumped to his feet when she appeared. "You look great."

Keegan felt her cheeks flush. "Thank you. Are you ready to get out of here? Do you want to go to your house and get changed?"

Rourk looked down at his day-old clothing and shrugged. "I guess I should."

Keegan looked over at her father. "Tell mom, we are going out and we'll be back later tonight. I doubt we'll be home for dinner. We have a date tonight." Keegan wrapped her arms around Rourk's waist and squeezed him tightly.

"Have fun." Her father turned back towards the TV.

Keegan grabbed a coat from the closet. "We'll drive to Nashville to get the computer. The stores are better, and they have better restaurants."

"Whatever you want is fine with me."

When they walked into Rourk's house, Keegan was surprised how comfortable and homey it felt. "Have I been here before?"

"Yes, when you picked me up to go away for the weekend. To the cabin. I'll be right back."

Keegan was amazed at how quickly Rourk showered and changed. *Must be nice to be a guy*, she thought. *They don't have to worry about make-up or what to wear.* He was even sexier than normal fresh out of the shower, with his hair still damp and his shirt sticking to his chest. She couldn't keep her eyes off of him.

Rourk ran his hand through his hair subconsciously. "Is something wrong?"

Keegan waved a hand in front of her face. The room felt hot. "No, I just can't believe you're mine."

Rourk laughed. "I can't believe you feel that way." Rourk strode toward her and wrapped his arms around her. He pulled her tightly against him and bent down to inhale the scent of her hair. She had a woodsy sent about her that he found very sexy.

"We better get going. We have a long day of shopping ahead of us." Keegan grinned, squeezing him tight around the waist.

"Then we should go." With a smile, Rourk took her hand and led her out the door.

They merged onto the highway and passed beneath a large green sign for Nashville. Keegan was glad to see traffic wasn't bad at all, so it would be a quick drive. She loved going shopping.

"What kind of music do you like to listen to?" Keegan asked as she changed the stations.

Rourk shrugged. "I don't really have a favorite. Whatever you like is fine. I don't normally listen to music."

Keegan was aghast. "We are really going to have to lighten you up. Ok, well, what do you like to do with your free time?"

Rourk chuckled, then said, "I enjoy hiking, reading, running, shooting, training. You now the usual things."

Keegan crinkled her nose. "You sound like my brother. He's so boring."

Rourk laughed loudly. "I'm sure I'll have more excitement in my life now that you are part of it."

Keegan grabbed his hand and lightly traced her finger in circles on his skin. "I sure hope so."

They talked during the hour drive. Though, looking back, Keegan realized she did most of the talking, which seemed to be fine by Rourk.

When they got to the mall and found a parking spot, Keegan hopped out of the truck and said, "Ok. We have to go to the Apple store. My father will never let me live it down if you don't get a Mac."

"I'm clueless about computers," Rourk said honestly. "You can pick it out and I'll pay for it. I trust your advice."

"Sounds good to me." Keegan hurried forward, excited to get to the mall. She realized Rourk wasn't beside her, and twirled around. He was lagging behind, with his hands shoved in his pockets.

"Hurry up, slowpoke!" Keegan called, laughing.

Rourk shook his head, amused, and lengthen his stride to catch up with her.

For hours, Keegan dragged him into countless stores. Rourk spent at least a month of his military pay. He didn't mind at all.

Chapter 6

Today was their last day together at least for a few days.

Keegan felt sick to her stomach at the thought of leaving him. It didn't seem fair; they had just found each other.

As if he could read her mind, Rourk reached over and ran his hand through her hair. "It will only be a few days. I'll be coming to see you Friday night and we'll have all weekend together."

Keegan pouted. "That's so far away."

Rourk laughed. "It's not that far away. It's nothing compared to the year we spent apart."

Keegan's face fell and guilt flooded her. "I feel horrible that you were miserable for a year while I was out having fun with my friends."

"There is nothing to feel sorry for, Keegan. You didn't know. We can't change what the black magic did, we can only move forward." He kissed her gently on the lips. "It's the way of the elf. We weren't supposed to meet until we turned eighteen, anyway."

Keegan laid her head against him. "I guess you're right. It still sucks though."

Warrick ran into the room giggling and breaking their sorrowful silence. Keegan smiled and scooped him up. "You're going with me tonight. You better not throw a fit on the plane."

Her little brother stuck his tongue out.

Keegan laughed and put him back down. "Go play with your blocks or something."

As Warrick ran away, headed for the toys, Rourk stared after him with a smile. "It must be pretty neat to have siblings," he said.

Keegan heard the wistfulness in his voice. It had never occurred to her that Rourk was an only child and that it could be a lonely thing. To lighten the mood, she rolled her eyes. "That's one way to put it. Although, I have to admit it would be odd to be an only child. You must have been lonely growing up."

"I didn't know any better. Being alone was normal to me."

"Keegan, Rourk, come have some breakfast." Her mother peeked out of the kitchen. There was a streak of flour on her cheek that made Keegan laugh.

They walked to the table hand-in-hand.

"Are you packed? We have to leave by 3:00." Her mother stood at the stove, scooping the last remnants of scrambled eggs from the skillet. She looked at Keegan.

Keegan reached over and pushed some eggs on her plate. "No, but I'm only bringing my backpack so I don't really have much to pack. It will just take a few minutes."

"Do you mind if I drive you guys to the airport?" Rourk asked before taking a sip of his juice. "I'd like to spend as much time as possible with Keegan."

Emerald' eyes twinkled as she glanced over at him. "That would be nice of you. I'm sure Keegan won't object."

Keegan felt her face turning red. "Are you sure you need to come with me mom?"

"It's better to be safe than sorry. We're not sure how the distance will affect you. I have to run to the store today and get a rose quartz necklace for you. I'm going to charge it with healing energies and hopefully that will ease some of the discomfort."

Rourk finished chewing his toast, then said, "Having a healer in the family comes in handy."

"Yeah, especially when Keegan was little. She was quite the daredevil. I lost count of how many times I had to fix her up after one of her stunts." Her mother had a faraway look—a slight smile on her face as if she was visualizing a memory.

"I can picture that." Rourk squeezed her hand across the table.

"Come on Mom, I wasn't *that* bad."

"Whatever, Keegan." Emerald turned to lean against the counter and crossed her arms. "Then where did all the scars on your legs come from?"

Keegan looked down at her plate and shrugged. "Ok, maybe I was that bad."

"Where did you get that scar?" Rourk touched a long gash on her shin. His finger made her shiver.

"We were at a camp in Maine, and I thought the water was deeper than it was when I jumped off the dock. Turned out it wasn't very deep at all, and I landed on a huge rock."

Thaddeus walked in as she was speaking. When she finished, he said, "A dare devil klutz—quite the combination."

Keegan threw a biscuit at him, but Thaddeus just caught it and took a bite.

Rourk had stayed quiet during the exchange, watching them interact. "You guys have a great family. My house is always so quiet."

"Well, get used to it. You're part of the family now. Lucky you." Thaddeus smirked.

Rourk looked over at Thad with a serious expression on his face. "Thanks to you. I will forever be in your debt for bringing back our bond."

Thaddeus gave him an impish grin. "You might take that back after dealing with the drama queen for a while."

Rourk grinned and shook his head. "Somehow I doubt that." He paused, his eyes on Thaddeus's. "Seriously, thank you."

Thaddeus shrugged. "No problem."

Emerald set her mug down on the table. "What are you guys going to do today?"

Keegan looked over at Rourk. "Not sure. I guess just hang out around the house. Maybe we'll go for a hike. I also want to look online at the schools." Keegan turned towards Rourk. "Speaking of online, we need to set up your computer and make sure you know how to use it for our chatting. Come on, let's go to my room."

Emerald raised an eyebrow, but didn't say anything.

Rourk glanced around her room, taking it all

in. He noticed a picture of Keegan with the shapeshifter on her nightstand. Keegan caught his gaze. "Sorry." She leaned over and took the photo down.

Rourk took it from her hands and stared at. "You looked happy."

Keegan shrugged. "He's very funny, and we had been friends for years."

"That's what worries me. I'm not exactly fun, Keegan. I'm not known for my sense of humor. What if you grow bored of me?"

Keegan smiled and met his eyes. "I think you are the sexiest, most exciting man I have ever met. Just the thought of getting bored of you is laughable. You are an elfin warrior. How could you possibly be boring?"

Keegan loved the way his eyes crinkled when he smiled.

"I love you Rourk. I've never loved anyone else," she said softly.

Rourk needed to hear her say that. "Every day for the rest of my life, I am going to try to show you how much you mean to me."

Keegan walked over to where he was sitting on the edge of her bed. She bit her lip, reached over, and put her hand behind his head. Electricity shot through her when their lips met. She closed her eyes and enjoyed the sensations that rushed through her body. When they finally pulled apart. Keegan grinned. "Yeah, I don't think you have anything to worry about. Definitely not boring."

Rourk shook his head and laughed. "Let's get this computer set up."

Keegan pulled the new laptop out of the bag

and plugged it into the wall.

It didn't take too long to get the account set up, and Keegan showed him the basics of Skype. He didn't even have an email account, so she set that up as well. Who didn't have an email account these days? He did have a military account, but that didn't really count since they couldn't correspond that way.

"All done. We still have some time. What do you want to do?"

"We could go for a walk? We've been inside all day."

"Sure, want to go to my favorite spot? I'll bring my camera."

"I'd love to. Although I have been there many times already."

Keegan looked surprised. "Oh really?"

"Yes, when you used to think of me it would mentally beckon me. Many times I watched you taking photos or sitting on the rocks, thinking."

Keegan gave him a funny look. "You know that's pretty creepy."

"I know." His smile was chagrined. "I couldn't help it. I tried, I really did. I just couldn't stay away from you."

"Anyone else I would call the cops on." She held her hand out for him to grab. "However, since it's my fault for always thinking about you, I guess it's ok. I hope I didn't do anything embarrassing."

"Just make a few spills once in a while, which only made me crazier about you. You would always grin when you tripped."

"I've actually gotten much better with my balance since I started training with Thaddeus and my mother."

"Well, now you can train with me."

"I can impress you with my ninja skills." Keegan gave him a sly smile.

"Everything about you impresses me."

"See, that's why I love you so much." Keegan led him out of the room and down the stairs.

"Do you think we should pack a lunch?"

Rourk involuntarily flinched and tensed up as he recalled the memory of Keegan eating lunch in the woods with the shapeshifter. He needed to push all of that behind him and just look forward. The was no sense holding onto all of the jealousy he felt. "Sure, lunch sounds great. Do you need some help?"

"I got it." Keegan packed up their lunch and they went out for a couple of hours. Already the sadness was starting to set in at the thought of leaving Rourk so soon.

Keegan stopped to pick up a rock and Rourk continued on ahead. She tossed the rock back and forth between her hands as she watched him walk. His shoulders were so strong and broad... Grinning, she dropped the rock and ran up behind him and jumped on his back, latching on to him. Rourk laughed and spun her around.

Keegan kicked her legs. "Put me down."

"Nope, I'm carrying you the rest of the way. You don't weigh much more than a ruck-sack."

Keegan laughed. "Ok, but don't blame me when your back hurts."

They reached the creek and Rourk let her down.

The woods stretched around them and the creek twisted before them. Some of the trees were already bare, but many were still crowned by red and orange that lit like fire in the sunshine.

They walked to the edge of the crystal clear water, their shoes crunching on dried leaves. Keegan looked around, closed her eyes, and took a deep breath. "This is my favorite spot on earth." She grasped Rourk's hand, smiling. "Now I get to share it with you."

"Thank you. That means a lot to me."

"Do you have a favorite spot?" Keegan asked.

Rourk shrugged. "No, I just love being outdoors; it really doesn't matter where it is. I don't have a particular spot. Although, there is something about the Tennessee woods that makes me feel at home."

"Do you want to move back here when you are out of the Army?"

Rourk tilted his head and looked at her closely. "I figured we would move back here since your family is here. Is that what you want?"

Keegan thought about it for a minute. "Yes, I would like to come back here. As long as we can still travel."

Rourk turned to face her, cupping her face in his warm hands. "I would love to see the world with you."

Keegan just smiled, a flush covered her cheeks. She took the blanket from him and spread it over the ground, before pulling out the sandwiches and drinks.

"Sit down so we can eat." She gestured for him to sit next to her.

Rourk complied. He popped open a can of soda and leaned back on his hand. "Keegan, I have not felt this at peace in a very long time. It's almost too good to be true."

"Don't jinx us. This is wonderful, but I will be leaving in a couple of hours." She stared at him intently, memorizing the expression on his face. "I don't want to be away from you, Rourk."

Rourk leaned forward "I know. Just remember—I will be thinking of you every minute and counting them down until I can visit you."

They spent two hours relaxing by the creek and learning more about each other. Finally, it was time to pack up and head out to the airport.

Keegan felt a lump in her throat thinking about it.

Chapter 7

Keegan took a last look around her room, saddened to leave it again. It hadn't been that long since graduation, really. Not very long since she'd moved to Alaska. But it *felt* like ages. She hurt to leave her room behind. So many things had changed...

"Come on, Keegan, we can't miss the flight." Her mother yelled from downstairs.

"I'm coming!" she yelled back, exasperated. She grabbed her bag from the bed and hurried back down the stairs.

Rourk took the bag from her hand and threw it over his shoulder. Keegan smiled as she stared after him—she loved how broad his back was. He turned slightly and reached his hand out for her. She grabbed it and squeezed, feeling the connection from his body to hers.

Keegan jumped in his truck and scooted into the middle so she could be as close to him as possible. Her mother and Warrick were settled in the backseat. Warrick was already screaming because he didn't want to be buckled into the car seat.

Keegan laid her head on Rourk's shoulder and didn't speak for most of the ride. She was afraid if she talked about it, she would cry. There was no sense in making it harder on Rourk than it already was.

Keegan peeked up at Rourk and noticed his jaw was tense. She reached up and ran her finger along his jaw and smiled when he relaxed. They exchanged a quick glance, but neither of them spoke.

When they arrived at the airport, Rourk pulled into the garage and found a spot. While her mother wrestled with Warrick, Keegan and Rourk got their bags out of the truck.

The walk inside was just as silent as the drive. Keegan held Rourk's hand, her own palm sweaty and her heart aching at the thought of leaving him. Her mother was subdued as well.

Outside the security line, Rourk turned to Keegan with sad eyes. Emerald stepped away from them, making a show of fussing over Warrick so that they could say goodbye.

"I'll stay here till the plane leaves," Rourk said, touching his forehead to hers. "I wish I could go back and wait with you."

"Me too. I don't want to say goodbye." Keegan closed the space between them and flung her arms around his neck. She couldn't hold back the tears any longer.

"I will be there in a few days. It will go quickly." Rourk tilted her chin up so she could meet his eyes. His grey eyes looked pained.

Keegan rubbed her face with the sleeve of her jacket and tried to give him a smile. "I'm sorry. I promised myself I wouldn't cry. I'm such a baby sometimes."

Rourk gave her a sad smile. "Just a few days."

Keegan turned and walked towards the security line. She glanced back to find Rourk staring intently at her. He was breathtaking to look at. He stood as still as a statue, his eyes only on her.

She grabbed her phone from her coat pocket. *Miss you already xoxos*

She grinned when she saw him reach into his jeans and pull out his flip phone. A wide smile broke across his face. He looked so cute pecking away at the keyboard.

Miss you more. I love you Keegan don't forget that

Never. I love you 2 I'll text you when we land.

Thank you. I guess texting isn't so bad after all. Rourk replied.

They finally boarded the plane. Keegan felt a strong urge to run off the plane and back into Rourk's arms. Instead, she plopped into the seat and folded her arms across her chest. "This sucks."

"I know, honey. Here put this on before we take off." Her mother pulled a gaudy pink crystal necklace from her bag and held it out.

"Couldn't you have picked a better color? You know I don't look good in pink. And it's so clunky." Keegan grabbed it from her mom and smiled when she felt the energy radiating of it. "Wow, Mom, that's powerful."

"I had to use rose quartz. It's the love stone. I'm hoping that on top of the healing energies, it will keep the pain at bay. Here let me put it on you."

Emerald reached over to clasp the necklace around Keegan's neck. Warrick kept trying to pull it off. *This is going to be a long flight,* Keegan thought with a sigh. At least they were in first class so they had plenty of room.

She grabbed a magazine and started flipping through it. When she realized she wasn't even looking at the pages, she shoved it back in the pocket of the seat. She wondered if Rourk had left yet. Probably not. He would wait until the plane was in the air.

About thirty minutes later, they finally took off. Her mother kept glancing over at her, worry lines on her brow.

Keegan rolled her eyes. "I'm fine, Mom. I'll let you know if I feel any pain."

Her mother nodded and started quietly reading a book to Warrick. After a couple moments, he grabbed it from her hands and threw it across the seat. Her mom sighed and pushed a strand of hair behind her ear.

Warrick started crying and pulling on his ears. Keegan watched as her mom placed her hands over his ears and the crying stopped instantly. Keegan secretly wished she had been born a healer. Her power of invisibility was cool and all, but she rarely got to use it.

The further they got in the air, the tighter Keegan's chest felt. She grabbed her mom's hand and squeezed it, gasping.

"How bad is it?" Her mom reached over,

placing a hand on Keegan's forehead.

"It's just in my chest. Feels funny, like a tightening."

"Not in your stomach?"

"No, just my chest." Keegan put her hand over her heart and grimaced. It felt like her heart was in a vise as it slowly cranked shut.

"Great, the necklace is working." Her mother smiled and sat back in the seat.

"What do you mean *great*? It hurts."

"I know it hurts," her mom whispered. "But I cannot heal the heart, you know that. This pain you just have to learn to live with."

"Wonderful." Keegan threw her head back against the seat.

"Just take some deep breaths and try to relax. Hopefully you can fall asleep. This is a long flight."

"Thanks for the reminder." Keegan stretched out her legs and turned her head to the side. "Let me see Warrick."

Her mother handed the baby over.

Keegan stuck out her tongue and made funny faces. Warrick giggled loudly when she acted like she was going to gobble up his hands. He eventually got tired and fell asleep, so Keegan handed him back to her mother, thankful he had been a distraction at least for a little while.

The pain in her chest hurt, but it was bearable. She closed her eyes and thought of Rourk. She was surprised that she could actually see him. He was walking around in his house packing his stuff. Keegan watched as he sat down on his bed and buried his head in his hands. Keegan's heart ached for him. She watched as he stood up and walked to the kitchen and grabbed a drink.

Keegan opened her eyes and shook her mom's arm. "Mom, I can see Rourk when I close my eyes."

Her mom smiled sleepily. "Of course you can. He is your chosen."

"But we're so far away. I thought that only worked when we were close by like at the house."

"No, you can see him anytime you close your eyes and think of him. Unless he decides to block you."

"Well, that's better than the webcam."

"Eventually your bond will grow stronger as time passes, and you can speak to each other with your mind."

"Seriously?" Keegan's eyes were wide.

"Yes, but it takes a lot of energy. Your father and I rarely do it unless something important is happening. It's just easier to pick up the phone and text." Her mom turned her head where it was against the headrest and eyed her. "Don't overuse the gift to see your chosen. Make sure you give him privacy. "

"I'll try, but it's so fun." Keegan closed her eyes again.

Rourk was now in the living room talking to his father. Keegan wished she could hear what they were saying. Rourk had his forearms resting on his knees and was leaning forward while his father talked. She watched as he stood up and walked into his room. He grabbed his backpack and headed towards the door. He walked out without turning to his father one last time. They must have already said their good byes.

Her mom shook her arm. "Keegan, I told you not to invade his privacy."

"What? I was just trying to sleep." Keegan said innocently.

"Sure you were," her mother said, shaking her head. "That's why you have a goofy grin across your face."

Keegan laughed. "He's just so cute!"

Chapter 8

Rourk was waiting to board the plane and he couldn't stop smiling. He leaned back in the hard plastic chair, not seeing anything around him.

All he could see was Keegan.

The bond had returned. He had really believed she was lost to him forever. Now, she was his once more and all they had to do was make it through this separation period. That would be easy compared to what they'd already been through.

Rourk hated to admit it, but he was upset that Keegan wanted to postpone their handfasting. It was tradition after all. When elf mates turned eighteen, they were wed—it was how it had always been and always would be.

However, at this point, he was willing to wait if that was what Keegan wanted. He just hoped nothing came between them again. He didn't think he could handle losing her a second time.

How did his father make it through the day

without his mother? The very thought of Keegan dying... Rourk couldn't even think about it.

His phone dinged in his pocket, and his heart dropped. Multiple scenarios of Keegan in pain flashed through his mind as Rourk fumbled to get his phone out of his pants. When he flipped it open, relief flooded his body.

Landed. I'm fine. The necklace worked.

The thudding in his chest calmed to a dull ache. Rourk took a deep breath and let it slowly before tapping out an answer. *That's great. I was worried.*

If I close my eyes I can see you :)

Rourk chuckled. *I know. You forget I feel a pull when you think of me.*

Ack! You knew I was watching you?

Well, I knew you were thinking of me.

Sorry, my mom says I should give you privacy.

He didn't think he could ever text as fast as she could. He typed his reply. *I don't mind. I love knowing I crossed your mind.*

A crackly voice over the loudspeaker announced it was boarding time for his flight. Rourk didn't want to say goodbye, even if it was only for a couple hours.

Gotta board plane. I'll text you when I land.

Ok. Love You xoxoxos

I love you.

Rourk took a deep breath and acknowledged the pain that tore through his chest. A reminder of their bond. A pain he would gladly bear.

Flipping his phone closed, Rourk stood and shoved it into his pocket. He walked to the counter, where he handed off his ticket to a slender brunette with an honest smile.

He had a long flight ahead of him, and he had to switch planes in Chicago. Thankfully, the first flight passed uneventfully and actually landed on time. He wasn't so lucky with the second flight, which was on a two hour delay—and almost stretched to three hours.

He sent Keegan a text. *Landed in Chicago.*

YAY! It's late here so going to head to bed soon. Text me when you get home so I know you made it safely.

Warmth flooded his body. It was something simple—just a girlfriend who wanted to know her boyfriend returned home safely. But it made him feel alive.

Ok.

Night xoxo

Goodnight.

Keegan held the phone to her chest and sighed.

She was propped against the headboard on her bed, sitting in the semi-darkness of her bedroom. A triangle of light spilled across the floor from the open bathroom door, illuminating the fluffy purple rug that covered the hardwood.

Her mom and Warrick were already fast asleep on the fold-out couch in the living room; she couldn't hear a peep from them. Her room felt quiet and empty. Something was always happening back home, with her parents constantly in and out and her brothers yelling and stomping around. Even knowing her mother was in the other room, Keegan still felt homesick.

Since she had been in the air all day, she felt kinda gross. She pulled off her sweater and stepped out of her jeans, throwing both on the floor. Keegan walked into her little bathroom and stood in front of the mirror beneath the harsh globe lights. She lightly touched the necklace and smiled. With her fingers still on the chain, she closed her eyes and searched for Rourk.

He was nodding off in a chair at Chicago O'Hare. Keegan recognized the airport from all the times her family had flown through it—it was one of the major international airports that had flights all over the world. Rourk was slouched so that his head rested on the back of the black chair, and his hands were clasped tightly over his chest. His military backpack rested between his feet.

Keegan felt a rush of pride. He was hers.

She opened her eyes with a sigh, and reached back to unhook the necklace. As soon as the chain fell from her fingers to the bathroom counter, searing pain rushed through her body. Keegan dropped to her knees with a cry, hanging on to the edge of the sink. She tried to reach for the necklace but the pain intensified. She curled into a ball on the cold tile floor and clutched her stomach.

"MOM!" Keegan screamed.

Her mother was by her side in an instant. Emerald immediately noticed the necklace on the bathroom counter and snatched it up. She dropped to her knees to clasp it around Keegan's neck. "Oh Keegan, I'm sorry. I should have warned you not to take off the necklace."

While Keegan cried silent tears and the pain subsided, her mom pulled a towel from the rack and covered her. Emerald wrapped her arms around Keegan and asked softly, "Are you ok?"

Keegan wiped her eyes and nodded.

"Are you still in pain?"

Keegan nodded again and wrapped her arms around her stomach, letting her weight rest against her mother. They sat silently for a moment, Emerald slowly rocking Keegan until she calmed down.

Emerald brushed Keegan's auburn hair from her face, then cupped her daughter's cheek as she said, "Put on some clothes and go lay on your bed. I will give you a full healing."

Keegan used her mother's hands as support so she could stand. She slowly made her way into the darkened bedroom and fumbled through her dresser for some pajamas. Each movement was painful. She stepped into her clothes as another tear left a cold trail down her cheek.

Keegan couldn't believe something as beautiful as their bond could cause this much pain. The pain had eased slightly once her mom put the necklace back on, but there was still a deep throbbing throughout her body.

Emerald put her arms around Keegan and guided her to the bed. "Close your eyes. It will be over shortly."

Keegan laid back on the soft bed and closed her eyes. She pictured Rourk as she took several deep cleansing breaths. Her mother's hands felt like they were on fire when she placed them over Keegan's stomach.

Despite the uncomfortable heat, it was as if her mother's hands were drawing all the pain out of her body. Keegan could feel it coursing beneath her skin and into her abdomen, where it disappeared into her mom.

Within minutes the pain was gone.

Keegan pushed to her elbows, trying to sit up.

"Shhh, stay still, Keegan," her mom chastised. "I want to give you a full healing. It will take another twenty minutes. Just lay there and relax."

Keegan must have fallen asleep, because the next thing she knew she awoke and her clock said it was 7:00 am.

Ugh, I do not want to get up and get ready for school, she thought irritably. The damn necklace was making her neck itch. It wasn't very comfortable to have a giant rocks hanging on her chest—especially sleeping with said giant rocks.

She stretched beneath her covers, putting off leaving the warmth of her bed for the cold of her room. Sounds from the kitchen indicated her mother was up and around, so Keegan finally headed for the bathroom.

After brushing her teeth and hair, she grabbed her black and white polka dotted robe and went out to the kitchen.

Her mother was sitting at the table, her fingers tapping gently on her steaming mug of tea. She was still in the sweats she'd slept in, her short hair sticking up wildly on her head. Emerald looked up, her brow furrowed in concern. "Feeling ok?"

Keegan shrugged, tugging her robe tighter. She slid into a seat at the small table. "Yeah, I feel fine. Just the throbbing pain in my heart. I guess I'll get used to it. That's nothing compared to the pain last night. I'm glad you were here."

"I'm sure you won't forget to leave the necklace on now." Her mom gave her a wry grin.

Keegan looked down at her chest and picked

up the crystal necklace, angling it to catch the early morning sunshine. She let it drop. "Mom, it's so ugly. Couldn't you have found something better looking? "

"No, I told you it had to be rose quartz. You are lucky I was able to find those stones and have the necklace made in such a short amount of time."

Keegan recalled the pain that ripped through her body. She looked over at her mom and quietly said, "Thank you."

"You're welcome. Do you want me to make you some breakfast before you go to class?"

"Sure. How long are you staying?"

"I was thinking I'll stay 'till Thursday since Rourk is visiting on Friday. I don't want to be in the way."

"That sounds good, Mom." Keegan smiled. She was really pleased to have her. "I'll show you around town when I get back from classes."

Emerald eyed her daughter. She cleared her throat and shifted in her seat. "Keegan, are you sure you don't want to tie the knot?"

Keegan fought the urge to roll her eyes. She really did understand why her family was so set on it—and Rourk too—but she had to be true to herself. "I'm sure. Not right now. Just give me some time. It's not like we are going anywhere."

"I'm going to start planning anyway," her mother said as she stood. She wandered to the fridge and pulled the eggs from it. "It will be fun. We can look at dresses if you want."

"What part of I'm not getting married anytime soon don't you get?" Keegan grumbled.

Her mother ignored her. "It takes forever to

find the perfect dress, and it's never to early to start. Plus, you know you love trying on dresses."

Keegan watched as her mom cracked several eggs into a large bowl and began whisking them. *How does she do it?* Keegan wondered, shaking her head. *I'm actually excited at the thought of trying on wedding dresses.*

She didn't want to admit defeat, but pretty dresses won *every* time. "Well, I guess it couldn't hurt to try on a few."

Her mother grinned. "It's settled, then. We'll look while I'm here."

"Shopping is pretty lame here, Mom. Trust me on this. Let's just wait 'til my next visit." Keegan jumped up to pour herself a glass of orange juice.

"Fine." Her mom sighed and poured the eggs into the pan.

Keegan took her glass of OJ and went back to her room to get her phone. She texted Rourk, but when five minutes passed and he didn't reply she figured he was busy training. She had to stop herself from closing her eyes and checking on him. This newfound gift was going to be hard to resist.

She refilled her juice back in the kitchen as her mom set the table for breakfast. Keegan had to admit it was nice to have her mother there to cook for her again. It was good to have the company.

"This is great, Mom." Keegan filled her plate with food and took a seat across from her mother.

"Glad you approve. Your brother doesn't seem to agree."

Keegan smiled warmly at Warrick as he tossed his eggs on the floor. "He doesn't know what he's missing."

There was no sound but for the clink of their silverware and Warrick's occasional laugh as he tossed more food beneath the table.

"Thanks for making breakfast," Keegan said when she was finished. She dumped her plate in the sink and kissed her mom on the forehead. "I need to go see if I can find something to wear that matches this necklace."

"It's not that ugly, Keegan. I think it's quite pretty."

Keegan raised an eyebrow and smirked at her mom. "Uh huh. Whatever you say, Mom."

In her bedroom, she stared into her closet and thought, *I need to go shopping.* Since she hadn't brought a lot of her wardrobe with her to Alaska, she was seriously lacking.

She decided on a white off-the-shoulder sweater. If she had to wear the necklace she might as well put it on display. She pulled out a pair of loose-fit jeans and slipped into them. What was she going to wear for shoes? She had to walk around campus so she decided on her frayed white Converse sneakers.

Keegan put on some light makeup. She liked the neutral look—a bit of pale, pink blush and shimmery eyeshadow with some clear lipgloss. Her mother always told her natural was best. She curled her hair in front of the bathroom mirror, leaving it to hang down in big waves.

Good enough, Keegan thought, unplugging her curling iron.

The dolphin earrings that Donald had given her for Christmas were resting on a corner of the sink. When she saw them, her heart felt heavy.

She wondered how he was doing and if he would ever talk to her again. It pained her that she had hurt him so deeply.

Thaddeus *did* say Donald would find someone else. That was one small ray of hope. Keegan was glad to know he would find happiness. He deserved to be happy.

Keegan enjoyed the time she spent with her mother and Warrick. The apartment was usually so quiet. Being able to come home from school and see them was wonderful.

They did some of the touristy things around town that Keegan had always wanted to do. Warrick loved the train ride up the mountain, where the snow was thick on the evergreen trees. Keegan took them to the wildlife sanctuary she had been volunteering for, where she introduced them to the staff and animals.

Her mother didn't care to have pictures taken, but Keegan made them humor her. She got some amazing shots of her mom and her brother. Alaska was a beautiful place for photography enthusiasts. She filled an entire memory card—it would keep her busy editing after they were gone.

When the time came for them to fly home, Keegan felt stronger with the underlying pain that came from the bond. Her mother's constant help and healing had prepared Keegan for her absence.

She was sad to see them go, but also excited.

Rourk would be there soon.

Chapter 9

Keegan woke up elated on the morning of Rourk's arrival.

As she stood before the bathroom sink brushing her teeth, she was stricken by the thought that for the first time, she and Rourk would *really* be alone. The idea made her shiver in expectation...and in nervousness.

Is today the day I lose my virginity? She thought as she tossed her toothbrush into the holder. Goodness! She certainly hoped so!

She wondered if she should go to the drug store and get some protection. Although, Rourk did seem like the kind of guy that would take care of something like that. Plus, it would be so embarrassing for her if she had to. She decided to leave that up to him.

Keegan tore through her underwear drawer trying to find something sexy. She laughed as she picked up her *Hello Kitty* underwear. That would not work. Maybe she should go shopping. It would give her something to do while she waited for him to arrive.

Yes, she thought, nodding to herself. She threw on pair of sweatpants and a *Save the Dolphins* t-shirt and drove to the mall.

If you could call it a mall. As she parked the Jeep in the nearly empty lot, she thought it looked more like a dingy strip shopping center. It was a large, yellow brick square with dirty glass doors and cracked sidewalks. Unfortunately, it would have to do. She had no other option.

There was a big department store, so she went there first. All the underwear seemed so adult. Either too sexy or too old looking. She picked up a pair of granny pants and stared at them in disgust. Finally, she decided on a pair of black boy shorts with matching bra. At least she would match. She couldn't wait to get home and try them on.

On second thought, she was already at the mall, so she might as well stop at Starbucks and get a white chocolate mocha. Keegan smiled and strolled down the hall looking in the windows but not really seeing anything. Only three more hours and Rourk would be there. She had butterflies in her stomach and couldn't seem to wipe the goofy grin off her face. People probably thought she was crazy, but she didn't care.

When she got home, she decided to take a quick shower. By the time she finished getting ready, it would be time to pick up Rourk from the airport. She grabbed her phone and texted Anna. *Ack Rourk will be here soon!*

YAY!

Have you heard from Lauren? She never

returns my texts anymore.

She hasn't been talking to me either, Anna replied.

Keegan stared at Anna's text, worried. *I hope she is okay.*

Maybe we can go visit her next week.

That would be cool. I can afford to miss a couple of days of classes. Actually, she would be happy to miss school.

Have fun with Rourk and I want DETAILS!

Of course. Xoxos. Keegan smiled when she hit send.

She turned the shower on as hot as she could stand it and stepped into the tub. The water felt great as it pelted her skin. She used her special scented soap: sandalwood and vanilla. She wanted to be perfect for Rourk.

The necklace felt so heavy and annoying in the shower. She had to remind herself to be grateful for it. Keegan lathered up her legs to shave while she was singing at the top of her lungs to one of her favorite Adele songs. She wished she had a voice like that girl—Adele sang like an angel.

She nicked herself as she was dancing. *Damn it! That's what I get for not paying attention.*

Keegan toweled herself off and pulled on her new underwear set. The bra had a bit of lace to it and the bottoms were just plain black. She twirled around in front of the mirror, checking herself at all angles. She shivered at the thought of Rourk's hands on her body. *How did I get so lucky?*

In her room, Keegan pulled out a dress she had found shopping with her mom. She had fallen in love with it when she saw it on the hanger. It was a v-neck dress with small ruffles down the buttons. Halfway down the fabric, there were cute ties on the side. She wanted the blue, but went with the gray, because it would match the necklace better. She pulled it over her head and brushed down the front to smooth it out. Keegan grinned and touched the little cap sleeves.

She looked over at the clock: one hour to fix her hair and makeup. She had put her hair in a bun in the shower so she didn't have to wait for it to dry. She sat down on her vanity desk and let her tangled mess of hair fall free from the bun. She smiled; she wouldn't have to do too much to her hair. It was nice and wavy from being wrapped up.

Keegan decided she didn't want to go overboard with the make-up. It seemed guys didn't like make up as much as girls did. Who would have guessed it? At least, that's what Donald and crew said. Keegan felt a pang of guilt when she thought of Donald. He always said she looked best without a trace of make up and her hair wild. He had always made her feel beautiful.

Keegan shook off thoughts of Donald, and went back to her make-up. When she was done, she had about twenty minutes left. She couldn't stand waiting in the silence of the apartment, so she grabbed her cardigan and went to the airport.

She couldn't wait to see his face; she was so tempted to try to visualize him in her mind. Her mother was right—it wasn't fair for her to check up on him all the time. Besides, she was going to have him there in the flesh in a few moments.

She parked the Jeep, jumped out, and

shuffled inside. She was lost in thoughts of Rourk, and slammed into an older guy who was walking out of the building.

"I'm sorry," Keegan told him with a slight smile.

He smiled back and said, "No problem."

She walked up to the board just inside the doors to see Rourk's arrival gate. His flight was advertised as Gate B6—and was on time—so Keegan took a deep breath and tried not to run in that direction.

In just a few moments, my chosen will be walking through the entrance, she thought. The airport was busy since it was a Friday evening, but Keegan found a bench and sat down, watching people greet each other. She realized she had forgotten her camera. She smiled. *Oh well, we will have a lifetime of photos ahead of us.*

Keegan felt the pain in her chest subsiding. He was closer. She stood up when she saw people coming through the gate. Her heart was pounding so fast. She scanned the crowd, searching for his face and her heart skipped a beat as his intense grey eyes met hers. He walked confidently towards her with his back pack slung across one shoulder. She loved the plaid shirt he had on over his plain blue t-shirt. He was wearing cargo pants and looked like a model out of an outdoor magazine.

She rushed forward as he approached and flung her arms around his neck.

Rourk laughed when she caused him to lose his balance. "I take it you are happy to see me?"

She pulled his head towards hers and kissed him lightly. "You have no idea. This week seemed to drag on. I couldn't get you out of my mind."

Rourk laced his fingers with hers and they walked outside. "Well, I'm here now. All yours for the weekend."

Keegan narrowed her eyes. "You better be all mine forever."

Rourk grinned and shook his head. "You know I am."

"Are you hungry? Do you want to go out to eat or just head to the apartment?" Keegan asked, her heart fluttering at the thought of taking him home.

"Let's just head to your place. It was a long flight. I can always cook us something to eat."

When they got to her Jeep, she handed Rourk the keys. "You can drive. You need to learn your way around since you will be visiting me so often."

Rourk grabbed the keys and threw his bag in the back seat. He had to push the seat back quit a bit. "You are tiny."

Keegan blushed. "Well, female elves aren't known for being huge."

"I think you are perfect." Rourk leaned over and kissed her softly. She loved how she felt when their bodies connected. She couldn't wait to get him back to the apartment.

Keegan caught him up on her visit with her mom. She pretty much chattered non-stop until they reached her apartment. Once they pulled in, Keegan suddenly felt shy and nervous.

Her hands shook a little as she unlocked the front door. She flung the door open and dramatically announced. "This is it! My first home of my own."

Rourk stepped through the doorway and looked around. The living room was brightly decorated, showing off Keegan's personality—which was a stark contrast to his plain room. He took in the black couch with purple and pink throw pillows in front of a big flat screen TV. The floors were hardwood with strategically placed throw rugs in bright colors. There was a lime green ball hanging down from the ceiling as the light. He really hoped she didn't plan to decorate their place like this.

"So what do think?" Keegan's face lit up and her eyes sparkled.

"It's interesting. It certainly looks like it belongs to you," he answered honestly.

Keegan clapped her hands together. "I love it. My mom and I had so much fun decorating."

"Where do you want me to put my bag?" Rourk asked.

"You can just leave it by the door or put it in my room down the hall."

Rourk tried to hide his surprise. He set the bag down by the door. He hadn't even thought of their sleeping arrangements.

"Do you want to eat first?"

"Sure, I'm hungry."

"Me too." Keegan opened the fridge. "How does a frozen pizza sound? We can watch TV and eat."

"That works. Do you need me to help with anything?"

"Nope. Do you want a soda?"

Rourk walked into the kitchen and took the can of soda from her hand and set it down on the counter. "I just want to look at you for a moment."

Keegan felt her face flush. "Umm, ok. That's kinda weird."

"I missed you so much." Rourk took his finger and lightly traced the side of her face, sending shivers through her body.

"Me too." Keegan's voice was barely over a whisper.

Rourk wrapped his arms around her and pulled her close. He laid his chin on her head and inhaled. "I love the way you smell."

Keegan wiggled to get her head out from under his chin and looked up at him. "I love you."

Rourk smiled, "You better get that pizza in the oven. I know you get cranky when you are hungry."

She swatted him on the arm. "Well, if someone hadn't come in and interrupted me." She pushed him out of the kitchen. "I'll be out in a minute."

Keegan watched him through the doorway while she unwrapped the pizza. She was afraid she was dreaming and someone was going to pinch her and she would wake up. It was all too good to be true. She threw the pizza in the oven and hurried out to join him on the couch. She didn't want to be apart from him, even momentarily.

She sat down and felt the electricity race through her body when her thigh touched his. She wanted to drag him into the bedroom, but figured she would let him make the first move. Instead, she reached down and grabbed the remote off the glass coffee table. "Do you want to watch anything in particular?"

Rourk shook his head no. "I don't really

watch TV."

"Well, you are in luck. How does a show about vampires sound?" Keegan laid her head on his thigh and kicked her feet up on the couch.

"Sure. Sounds good."

After they ate the pizza, and the show was over. Keegan felt butterflies in her stomach. It was time. She looked up at Rourk. "Are you ready to go to bed?"

Rourk glanced around. "The couch will be fine."

"The couch? You came all this way. I finally have a place to myself, and you want to sleep on the couch? No way! You are sleeping in my room."

Keegan pulled him up and lead him towards her room.

"Keegan, I don't think this is a good idea. I don't know if I can control myself around you."

"Who said you had to control yourself?" Keegan gave him a sly grin that she hoped looked sexier than it felt.

Chapter 10

Rourk tensed as Keegan lead him into her bedroom. *Why hadn't he thought of this? He had been so thrilled to spend time with her he hadn't even thought of sleeping arrangements. Maybe he should have stayed in a hotel.* He really didn't know if he had the self control to resist her. She was so incredibly sexy.

Keegan turned and grabbed his hands pulling him the rest of the way into her bedroom. Rourk glanced over at the huge bed that took up most of the room. She slid her arms around his waist and smiled sweetly up at him. The electricity coursed through his body. Keegan took a couple steps backwards, pulling him with her, and then fell back on the bed giggling.

Rourk stared down at her. She was biting her lip and looking up at him expectantly. He closed his eyes and let the tension release from his body as he leaned down and got lost in her kiss. Keegan ran her hands through his hair and the kiss intensified. Rourk broke away and Keegan pulled him back for more. His mind screamed stop, but his body wouldn't listen.

She lifted up his shirt and ran her fingers up his chest. Rourk couldn't breathe.

"Keegan, don't." He pushed her hand back down.

She looked surprised. "What did I do wrong?"

Rourk rolled over to the side. "You didn't do anything wrong. I just don't trust myself."

"What do you mean you don't trust yourself?"

"Keegan, I want you so badly. I don't think I can stand being alone with you like this." He ran his hand through his hair, his brow knitted together. He couldn't meet her eyes.

"I want you too, so there *is* no problem." She reached for him again and he pulled away. Keegan sat up as Rourk stood beside the bed.

"It's against tradition. I know it's old fashioned, but I strongly believe in tradition." His voice was absolute.

Keegan's eyes widened. "You are my chosen. We're bonded, so it's ok. I want this, Rourk." She reached out for him. "I want you."

"We're not married. Why do you think elves get married so soon after they are bonded?"

"I don't know. I never really thought about it." Keegan flopped back onto the bed and rested her head on her hand.

"Keegan, I'm sorry. I can't. I know you want to hold off on the handfasting and I can accept that. However, you have to accept that we will not have sex until we are married. This is really important to me."

She sucked in her breath. "Are you serious? I

bought matching underwear today. I can't believe you are turning me down."

"I'm not turning you down. Don't be ridiculous. I want you more than I've ever wanted anything in my life. I would marry you right now, and spend all weekend in bed with you."

Keegan sat up and pulled her knees to her chest, wrapping her arms around them. "I don't want to get married just to have sex. I'm still not ready to get married."

"You know I will wait forever for you." Rourk reached over and tucked a strand of hair behind her ear. "You just tell me the date and time and I will be there."

Keegan wiped a tear from her cheek.

"Why are you crying?" His voice sounded panicked. "I don't want you to cry."

"I don't know. It's stupid. I was excited and nervous thinking I was going to lose my virginity today, and now I feel like an idiot. My own chosen doesn't want me." Keegan threw a pillow across the room, her anger obvious.

Rourk was worried she would turn the room into a block of ice. "Keegan, look at me."

She slowly raised her head to meet his eyes, a sullen look on her face.

"I'm sorry you don't agree, but this is who I am. You say that you love me right?' Rourk asked gently.

Keegan nodded.

"Well, you need to love this part about me as well." Rourk reached out to take her hand. "We have a lifetime to spend together, and I'm sure plenty of it will be spent in bed. Let's just spend this time getting to know each other more. Ok?"

Keegan wiped her nose with the back of her hand and nodded. "Will you still sleep in my bed with me?"

Rourk hung his head. "I can't. I'm sorry."

"I promise I won't attack you in the middle of the night."

Rourk took a deep breath. "I hope I don't regret this. Yes, I'll stay in here."

"Thank you. I'm going to change into my PJ's I'll be right back." Keegan rummaged through her drawer looking for the least sexiest thing to wear and then headed to her bathroom. She came out a few minutes later wearing Power Puff Girls pajamas. "How's this?"

"You look adorable." Rourk noticed she still had the necklace on. "Come here."

Keegan walked over and Rourk stood up. He put his hands around her neck to unlatch the necklace. Keegan jerked away. "No, don't take it off. It hurts too much."

"Keegan, I am here you don't need it anymore."

She looked skeptical. "Are you sure?"

"Trust me." He unlatched the necklace and set it on her nightstand.

Keegan grinned. "No pain." She reached up and kissed him. Rourk hesitantly returned the kiss.

"Don't worry, Rourk. I promised, so you need to trust me." She kissed him again.

"It's not you I don't trust, it's me. This is much harder than you can imagine. I've lain awake many nights dreaming of being alone with you."

"You have? Seriously?" She crossed her arms

across her chest. "You're not just saying that to make me feel better?"

"Of course not, Keegan, you are beautiful and you are mine. I want to explore everything about you. I just want to wait until you are my wife."

"That's really sweet." Keegan pulled his hand to her lips and kissed it.

"I know you're tired after that long flight. Why don't you get changed and we'll try to get some sleep." She crawled under the covers.

Rourk left to grab his backpack from the living room. He changed into a pair of shorts and T-shirt. He wished she would just agree to marry him so they wouldn't have to deal with this. It was almost funny—Keegan had been torturing him since he first laid eyes on her. He should be used to it by now. He would endure anything she threw his way.

He got under the covers and she snuggled up against him. She fit perfectly in his arms.

Rourk ran a hand through her hair, his other arm tucked tightly around her small frame. She was asleep in no time. He lie awake awhile, listening to her breathe. His last thought before he dozed off was *I am the luckiest man on the planet.*

Chapter 11

Keegan woke up and flung her arm across the bed to find it empty. *Was her night with him a dream?*

She rubbed her eyes and sat up, the blankets falling away from her. She looked around for any proof that he had been there, but saw nothing but the faint indentation in her purple satin sheets. She flopped back on the bed and grabbed the pillow next to her. Bringing it to her face, she pressed its softness to her face and breathed deep. *Yep, he's real.* She loved the smell of him—he smelled like the woods.

But where is he? She jumped out of bed and tugged her favorite robe from the hook over her door. It was a fluffy lavender robe from Target that had been worn so many times the elbows were going thin, but she loved it. She stepped into some slippers and went to search for him.

Love swelled in her chest as she stopped at the doorway of the kitchen. The early morning sunshine slanted through the window and illuminated him. His hair was mussed from sleep, sticking haphazardly up, and he was in a pair of sweatpants and a t-shirt. Keegan had never known him in such an intimate aspect.

Rourk was hovering over the coffee pot. He jabbed at a button; then, he frowned and punched another. When nothing happened, he swore under his breath and jerked the coffee pot out, glaring at it.

Keegan smirked and shook her head at his troubles with the coffeemaker. She closed her eyes and called on the power inside her. The tingling sensation that accompanied her main power of invisibility rushed through her body: starting from her head and claiming her body all the way to her toes. She loved to sneak up on people.

She tiptoed forward until she was right behind him.

"Need some help?" she asked and was disappointed when he didn't jump.

"I didn't hear you." Rourk turned wide eyes in her general direction. His brow furrowed as he searched the room for her.

Keegan let go of her power, and her body shimmered back into view. "I would hope not. What would be the fun in being invisible if you could be heard?"

His smile was huge. "I've never seen you use your power. Do it again."

She closed her eyes, relishing the familiar sensation as it ran through her body, and she was gone.

Rourk laughed. "Ok, you can come back now.

I'm impressed."

When she appeared beside him, Rourk turned and grabbed her around the waist. "I wasn't sure you were ever going to wake up. It's almost 9:00."

Their lips touched lightly, and Keegan felt hot and restricted beneath her robe. She stepped away. "What time did you wake up?"

"Five-thirty. Same time I usually wake up."

Keegan crinkled up her nose. "Yuck. I can't believe you willingly get up that early on a weekend. What have you been doing?"

"Not much. I stayed in bed for awhile. Then I figured I'd come see what you had to make for breakfast. However, I can't seem to figure out this thing." He gestured to the coffeemaker where it sat innocently on the counter.

She reached over and flipped a switch on the side, and it started making noise. "That's because it's set to automatically go off at 9:30 on the weekends. I like to wake up to the smell of coffee."

"That is a great smell to wake up to," Rourk agreed, pulling her close once more. This kiss was tender and slow, and he tangled his hands in Keegan's long hair, drawing it out. When he finally pulled away, he murmured, "How does french toast sound?"

"Yummy, that's one of my favorites." Keegan rubbed her hands together.

As he opened the fridge to pull out the eggs and milk, Keegan took a seat at the table, tucking her legs underneath her as she watched him. He turned on the stove and cracked a couple eggs in a bowl, then said, "Do you have any plans for us today?"

"Yes, we're going to pick out our puppy. I found a local breeder."

Rourk chuckled, whisking the egg mixture with a fork. "I almost forgot about the bulldog."

"I can't believe you already forgot about a member of our family." Keegan placed her hand to her chest in mock surprise. "We aren't going there till three so I thought I could show you around town, and where I go to school."

"I'd love to see where you have been spending your days." Rourk dipped a piece of bread in the mixture and slapped it in the pan. It started sizzling on contact.

"We might even get lucky and see the northern lights while you're here." Keegan's eyes lit up. "It's the most amazing thing I have ever seen in my life. Wait until you see the pictures." She paused. "Actually, you should see them in person. If we don't see them this weekend, I'll show you the pictures."

"That is something I would like to see," Rourk replied. He flipped the three pieces of toast cooking in the skillet and glanced at her.

Keegan stood and held up a finger as she walked backwards for the door. "I do have something to show you though. I'll be right back." She banged into the door frame and made a face, rubbing her elbow.

Rourk laughed.

"Not funny." She stuck her tongue out. She found the brown leather album on the desk in her living room. It was thick—much thicker than Keegan had meant for it to be.

She brought it back to the kitchen and placed it on the table. "These are the photos I've been saving for you. I took them with the lens you gave me."

Rourk brought her a plate of french toast and a mug of warm syrup. He sat down across from her and reached for the album. Slowly, he turned the pages and took in parts of Keegan's life he had missed.

Keegan reached over him and pointed at a photo. It was a close-up of dark gray rocks; the power of the lens allowed the droplets of water on the surface to stand out. Speaking through a mouthful of toast, Keegan said, "Those were taken at my favorite spot with the fisheye lens."

"They're beautiful, Keegan. You are really talented." He turned the page.

Keegan pointed with her fork at the page he was on. "That's a bunch of graduation and prom pictures. I had my mom take some for you."

Rourk looked over at her, one of his hands splayed across a picture of Keegan in her slinky gray prom dress. "So you took all of these photos especially for me?"

"Yeah, it was my father's idea."

"Keegan, this is an amazing gift." Rourk's voice was soft and full of emotion. "It means so much to me, knowing you were thinking of me as these photos were snapped."

He turned his smoky eyes to hers, and she thought he had the most intense eyes of anyone she had ever met. Keegan knew he meant everything he said one hundred percent. "I'm glad you like it. Why don't you finish making your breakfast and then we can see the rest?"

After Rourk had his own plate, Keegan paged through the album and told him about each photo as he ate his food. When she closed the last page, both of their plates were empty.

Rourk cleared his throat. "Thank you."

Just those simple words coming from him made her feel so happy. She reached across the space between them and ran her fingers through his hair. "You're welcome."

"I'm surprised you are not going to school for photography. Those shots are amazing."

Keegan sighed, dropping her hand to her lap and fiddling with the drawstring on her robe. "I've been seriously considering changing my major and going to an art school for photography."

"Why don't you?"

"Well, I've dreamed of being a marine biologist since I was old enough to know what one was," she said simply and shrugged. "I feel like I'll let my parents down if I don't go through with it. I really do love science and marine life. It's just not as much fun as I expected."

Rourk took her hands into his. "You should do what makes you happy. Your parents would not be disappointed as long as you were doing what you wanted to do."

"I've actually been looking into art schools in Seattle. I'm just not sure. I think I'll feel like a failure if I don't finish my biology degree." His hands were so much larger than hers; they were so much more creased and calloused.

"That's silly, Keegan. You can always do both if it's that important to you."

Keegan let go of his hands and pulled at her sleeves. "What I would really like to do is photograph animals. I would love to get some underwater photos of dolphins and other marine life." She shrugged. "That's probably silly."

Rourk reached over and pulled her into his lap. He swiped one hand through her hair, his skin warm as he rested his palm against her cheek. "It's not even slightly silly. I think that is an amazing idea. You could get the best of both worlds."

"You really don't think it's crazy?" She bit her lip, one hand playing with the hem of his T-shirt. Her heart thudded as she waited for his answer. His opinion meant so much to her.

"I really don't. But, it's your choice, so you need to decide what is best for you."

Keegan grinned. "Well, the photography program is much shorter. Which means we could get married sooner."

"I'm not going to lie. I like the sound of that." Rourk kissed her, a slow, lingering touch of his lips. When he pulled away, he caught her eye and said, "Whatever you decide, I'm beside you."

Wrapping her arms around his neck, Keegan squeezed. She was embarrassed to find she was a little teary-eyed. She took a deep breath, drawing in Rourk's earthy smell. His hair was like satin on her cheek.

I'm so lucky to have him.

Keegan took a deep breath and pulled back with a smile. "I'm going to get ready. I'll be back in a little while."

"How long are you going to be?" Rourk asked.

"Total? About an hour. It takes girls a little longer to get ready," she teased, and then winked at him.

"Ok, I'm going to throw on some clothes and go for a run. I'll be back in about 45 minutes."

Rourk kissed her one last time before she stood up.

Keegan rocked back and forth on her feet, her hands clasped in front of her, as she watched him walk away. She felt so at peace with him around. Once he walked out the door, she headed for the shower.

Keegan pulled the Jeep into the driveway of a large, red-brick home with a huge fenced-in yard. The shutters on every window were black, and the front door was framed by tall bushes shaped into spirals. She jumped out and pocketed her keys, then met Rourk at the front of the vehicle.

"I'm a little nervous. This is our first big purchase as a couple." She grasped his hand and squeezed it. "The house looks nice. I'm sure they take good care of the puppies."

"I've always wanted a dog. Not sure I would have picked a bulldog though." He laughed, tucking Keegan's hand into the crook of his arm as they began walking up the driveway. "Aren't they supposed to be lazy?"

"Hey, don't talk about Santa like that. Lazy is good! I just want someone to keep me company when I'm alone. We can always get a more active dog later, if you want. I'm sure he'll want a friend."

They mounted the three steps to the porch and came to a stop on a generic black and brown "Welcome" mat. Keegan reached over and rang the doorbell.

A woman who looked to be in her mid-forties open the door and greeted them with a warm smile that reached her pale blue eyes. "You must be Keegan and Rourk. Come in."

They stepped inside, and the woman closed the door behind them. Keegan glanced around in awe—the house was beautiful. The foyer ceiling soared above their heads, where a large, crystal chandelier hung down past the white railing of the upstairs balcony. To either side, arched doorways opened into equally large and open rooms: One filled with over-stuffed couches and chairs in warm, neutral tones and the other with a long dining table covered in fine China. It felt warm and inviting.

"The puppies are in the back room," their hostess said with another eye-crinkling smile. "And I'm Marjorie, in case you didn't remember."

"It's a pleasure to meet you, Marjorie. I'm Rourk,"—he put an arm around Keegan—"and this is Keegan."

The house was decorated in an understated, simple way. Lots of browns, reds, and gold made it look like a page out of a magazine. They passed through a huge kitchen filled with all stainless-steel appliances. It smelled like cinnamon which made Keegan hungry.

Marjorie came to a stop in front of a gated doorway. She unlatched the small wooden gate to let them pass through.

It was a small spare bedroom with hardwood floors and a single twin-sized bed covered in a plain white blanket. Six bulldog puppies, shaped like sausages and in a variety of colors, were wrestling on the floor.

"Oh my goodness!" Keegan clapped her hands together. She got on her knees and picked up an all-white bulldog, then kissed its face. His fur was so soft, and he had that adorable puppy smell—a sharp tang. She glanced at Rourk. "How are we ever going to choose?"

Rourk was still standing in the doorway. He chuckled and shrugged.

"Get over here!" Keegan teased him. She picked up a second wiggling bulldog—white and covered in black spots—and squeezed both puppies to her chest. "Which one do you like best?"

Rourk sat down beside her on the floor and gently took one from her. It squirmed in his grasp, trying to get it's little head around so it could nibble on Rourk's fingers. "They are all pretty cute. Do you like the ones with colors or the all-white ones?"

"Well, I always wanted one with different colors..." Keegan trailed off, eyeing the spotted one in Rourk's lap. The one she still held licked her face, its tongue wet and scratchy. Keegan giggled. "But the white one is super-cute, and he seems to like me. Is it a boy?" She held the puppy up and looked at its belly. "Oh shoot, it's a girl. Do you think we could name a girl Santa?"

"I think you can name a dog anything you want to name it." Rourk reached over to scratch behind the little dog's ear. She kicked her arms and legs as if she were trying to get to him. "Although, I don't think the name matches the dog. She should have a cool name like Athena."

"Hmm, Athena. I actually love that! I think she likes you," Keegan said as she handed the dog to him.

"I think we should take this one home," Rourk declared and looked the puppy in the face, inspecting it. She had dark eyes that were nearly hidden in the rolls of her face, and her nose was pale pink. Rourk laughed when she put a paw on his nose and licked him. "It's so fat and wrinkly."

Keegan stood up and brushed off the seat of her pants. She turned to Marjorie, who was watching from the doorway. "We would like to take this one. I wish we could take them all."

The woman smiled as she leaned to take Athena from Rourk's hands. "I understand. It's heartbreaking for me when they leave us, but the people who get them give the puppies the love they need. You picked a good one. This one has a great personality."

"She had her 9 weeks shots just last week, so you'll need to take her for the 12 weeks soon." Marjorie passed Keegan a computer print-out. "Here's the vet information, as well as what kind of food she's been eating."

They thanked her and paid for the little dog, then left.

Keegan held Athena snugly against her chest as they walked for the car. In the cold air, her cheeks were rosy and her eyes were twinkling.

"I love seeing you so happy," Rourk murmured, snaking an arm around her shoulders.

"I am happy. I'm not sure I have ever been this happy in my life." Keegan glanced up at Rourk's thoughtful face. "I know it sounds corny, but I've always felt something was missing until you."

"I feel the same way." Rourk kissed the top of her head.

As Rourk made to get in on the passenger side of the car, Keegan stopped him. She grinned sweetly. "I really want to hold Athena. Will you drive?"

"Of course." He shook his head, amused, and switched sides.

They made a quick stop at Petsmart to pick up all the necessities, plus a few extra toys. While they shopped, people kept stopping to stare at Athena, and asking if they could pet her. You would have thought she was a super model with all the attention she received.

"This puppy is going to be spoiled," Keegan said wryly as Rourk piled their bags into the back of the Jeep. "We might have gone a little overboard."

Rourk scratched Athena's head, earning a kiss in return—from the puppy and from Keegan. "She's worth it."

They walked into Keegan's apartment with the new addition to the family, and Keegan put her down on the floor as Rourk locked the door behind them. Athena ran around sniffing and checking out the place. Keegan followed her into the kitchen, where she checked out the stove, then slipped under the table. A second later, she shot from beneath the table and into the living room, her toenails scrabbling for purchase on the hardwood. Athena did three quick circles and went to the bathroom. On the rug. Rourk laughed, and Keegan rushed around trying to clean it up.

Soon after, the puppy fell asleep in front of the fireplace.

Keegan wrapped her arms around Rourk's waist, and they watched the little dog snore away.

"I'll make us some hot chocolate. It's so cold here," Keegan said with a shiver, and then shuffled off to the kitchen. She smiled when she pulled out the Godiva hot chocolate—it always made her think of her mother. Her mom loved to make the hot chocolate on cold days.

"Marshmallows?" she asked as Rourk came in the room.

"Of course." He grinned. He took a seat at the table.

Keegan put the saucepan on the stove and poured a generous portion of milk into it. She turned up the heat and left it to boil as she measured out the cocoa powder into two mugs. She could feel Rourk's eyes on her the entire time.

What a perfect day. She got to spend it with Rourk, and now they had a pet to make it even more complete.

"Do you think she'll like it here? With us?" Keegan asked, leaning her hip on the counter next to the stove. The milk was just beginning to bubble.

Rourk cocked his head. "Athena?"

"Yeah. What if she doesn't like us?"

"Athena will love you," he answered, his voice heavy with emotion. "And she already likes it here—she fell asleep."

Wrinkling her nose, Keegan said, "So? What does that have to do with it?"

"When an animal feels comfortable enough to fall asleep somewhere, it means they're happy." Rourk smiled. "It's the same as humans. Don't you sleep best at your parents' house?"

Keegan turned off the heat, thinking about his words. She poured milk into both mugs and stirred. "I suppose you're right."

"It's true."

Keegan dropped in some marshmallows and carried the mugs to the table, sitting down across from him. She wrapped her hands around her hot chocolate and felt the warmth radiate through her body. "Tonight, we'll take her out to look for the northern lights. Maybe she will bring us good luck."

They both smiled at Athena, who was still snoring away in the living room.

Later that evening, they drove out about an hour into the woods to a spot in the wildlife sanctuary where Keegan volunteered. It was the best spot to see the northern lights, according to all of the people Keegan worked with at the sanctuary. She'd checked online, and chances were good the lights would make an appearance that night.

When they pulled up to the park ranger's checkpoint, an older man with dark gray hair popped out of the booth and strolled up to the Jeep. Keegan rolled down her window, and Athena went crazy in Rourk's lap. "Hey, Roger. How'd the tours go today?"

The man gave her a crooked smile that deepened the age lines in his face. "Wasn't the same without you. You have a way with the kids."

"Giving tours is my favorite part," Keegan told Rourk. "I love interacting with the guests."

"And she's the best we've got, too," Roger said brightly, tipping his wide-brimmed hat up and squinting into the dim car.

"I'll be in on Tuesday." Keegan turned in her seat and gestured to Rourk and the puppy. "I want you to meet Rourk, and our newest addition, Athena."

"Pleasure to meet you, sir," Rourk answered politely.

Roger reached through the window to shake Rourk's hand. "Nice to meet you. Keegan talks about you all the time. It's nice to put a face to the name." He dropped a quick pat to Athena's head; her stubby tail wagged so fast it moved her whole body. Roger chuckled, then reached up and took off his hat. "You're a lucky man, Rourk. Keegan's a great kid. She never complains, no matter what chore we throw at her."

Rourk nodded his head in agreement. He was well aware of how lucky he was.

"We're hoping to catch a glimpse of the lights," Keegan told Roger excitedly.

"It's a good night for it. Have fun." The ranger turned and walked towards his four-wheeler, parked next to the checkpoint booth. He gave them a hearty wave, then revved the engine and wheeled away.

Keegan drove down a winding dirt road for several minutes before she finally pulled into a clearing in the woods. As she put the car in park, Rourk snapped Athena's tiny leash onto her new purple collar.

"I really hope the lights decide to show themselves tonight," Keegan said quietly. It truly was a breathtaking sight, and she wanted to share it with Rourk.

"Even if they don't, it's been a great day with you anyway," Rourk answered as they climbed from the car. He put Athena down and she promptly did her business in the grass.

"You're right," Keegan said with a sad smile. She stopped to praise Athena, handing the puppy a small treat from her pocket.

They held hands as they walked towards the picnic tables barely visible at the tree-line.

"You really enjoy working here, don't you?" Rourk glanced over at Keegan's face in the darkness.

"I love it. Not all of it is fun, but I know it's all worthwhile to preserve the land and help the animals."

"It's admirable." He held her hand as Keegan climbed onto the top of the table, then placed Athena in her lap before sitting beside her.

A burst of green lights lit up the sky, followed by splashes of pink and purple. Keegan gasped— she never got sick of it. Rourk's strong hand wrapped around her own, and they watched as random ribbons of color danced in the sky.

"It's beautiful. I've never seen anything like it." Rourk's eyes were locked on the skyline.

"I know. It's incredible. What an amazing world we live in," she said wistfully, as she laid her head on his shoulder and pulled the little wrinkled bulldog closer on her lap.

The weekend passed in a blur. Keegan wanted to cry when Rourk placed the necklace around her neck. "I'm not ready for you to leave."

"I know. I'll be back in a few days." Rourk leaned down and kissed the top of her head.

"How are we going to make it through this? It seems cruel."

He gave her a sad smile. "We'll just take it one day at a time. We have the computers; that helps."

"It's not the same." She threw her arms

around him and laid her head on his chest. His heartbeat was loud and steady.

"It's time to go." His voice sounded hoarse.

The drive to the airport was long and rough. Keegan tried to not let him see her cry—she didn't want it to be any harder for him than it already was.

After they said their good-byes, Keegan sat in a chair at the security checkpoint for over an hour. When the pain started in her chest, she knew he was gone.

Chapter 12

Rourk woke up before his alarm went off. His first thought was *Keegan*—the same thing he thought every morning. There was a four hour time difference, so she was most likely fast asleep.

He closed his eyes and thought of her, then smiled. She was curled up in her bed with the covers tucked under her chin. Her hair was a mess, tangled and spread across her pillow. She looked so peaceful with Athena curled into a little white ball at her side.

They were together again; he had to remind himself everyday. It was unbelievable—all those months of pain without her were suddenly history. Rourk gazed longingly at her for just a moment longer, then snapped opened his eyes.

He could watch her all day, but he knew it was wrong to invade her privacy like that. Gathering some clothes, he went to take a shower.

When Rourk finally sauntered from his room, Tommy was waiting outside.

"Hey, man," Rourk said, clapping his friend on the shoulder. "Good to see you."

Tommy raised an eyebrow and leaned away. "What has you so chipper? I've never seen you this happy."

"I met a girl." Rourk grinned. *That's the understatement of the day*, he thought wryly.

"Seriously? What's she like? When can I meet her, and most importantly—does she have a sister?"

Rourk laughed. "She is perfect. You'll be able to meet her soon enough. No, she doesn't have a sister, just two brothers."

"Figures." Tommy sighed. "What about friends?"

Rourk knew his friend was obsessed with meeting a new girl. He'd never known anyone to have such bad luck as Tommy. It wasn't that he was a bad-looking guy—average, really. He was tall and lanky with pale blond hair, blue eyes, and freckles across the bridge of his nose. But, what did Rourk know about girls and their tastes?

"I'm sure she has some friends."

"How did you meet her?" Tommy narrowed his eyes. "You're not exactly smooth with the ladies."

"She's from the town where I grew up. I've liked her for a long time, and she finally noticed me."

Tommy slapped him on the back. "That's great man. I'm happy for you."

"Thank you. I know you two will get along great. She'll be going to school in Washington."

"Really? So she probably does have some cute college friends." Tommy stroked his chin as if he were deep in thought.

It was time to change the subject. If he didn't, Tommy would go on about his lack of a girlfriend all morning.

"I'm looking forward to getting out of here and onto a team," Rourk said, shifting his rucksack on his back. The days of training had started to drag, and he was ready for a new start.

"Me too. The training is cool and all but..." Tommy shrugged. "I'm ready to move on. Plus, there aren't that many hot chicks around here. At least, any that aren't already married."

So much for changing the subject.

"We don't have much longer. We'll get a lot of time off for the holidays, so it will pass quickly. I'm hoping we're there by the New Year. Are we still going to get a place together?" Rourk glanced over at Tommy as they finally headed down the hallway.

"Of course! I've been looking online. We can get a sweet place between both of our housing allowances. I'm talking a pool, Jacuzzi, gym, bike trails, you name it."

Rourk shook his head. "I'll leave that up to you."

"I won't let you down. See you at lunch." Tommy headed off in the opposite direction.

Rourk was thinking of Keegan as he strolled towards the compound. He missed her so much. He missed her smell, her smile, her kiss... Thoughts of her consumed his mind—he needed to compartmentalize so he could focus at work.

He frowned when his phone vibrated in his pocket. He flipped it open and read *TOMMY*.

It was from Thaddeus.

Thaddeus, his future brother-in-law, was a psychic and rarely tried to step in and change fate. It was forbidden for those with the gift of sight. So if Thad was warning him, Tommy must have been in terrible danger.

Shit. Rourk clicked number three on his speed dial and pressed the phone to his ear. It just rang and rang. His heart thudded in his chest. He couldn't stand the thought of something happening to Tommy.

Rourk took off in a sprint towards the engineer department. He tried Tommy's number again. Still no answer. Soldiers stared at Rourk as he sprinted past, but he barely noticed. He skidded to a stop and glanced around; he was on Tommy's usual path to work. *Where was he?* Rourk dialed again and listened to the ringing. *Come on, pick up.*

The screech of brakes sounded like a gunshot in the morning, followed by a sickeningly loud *thump.*

"No!" Rourk screamed. He raced forward as fast as he could, and ran around the large brick building that separated him from the street.

Tommy was lying on the ground. A large white truck was stopped in front of him. Not a dent on the truck, but Tommy was crumpled on the asphalt. Two guys were kneeling next to him. Someone yelled "Call 911! Get a medic out here now!"

Rourk felt like he was walking through water as he made his way forward. Tommy was his only friend—he couldn't bear it if something happened to him. Something he could have prevented. He hadn't reacted quickly enough—he had failed.

Thaddeus had trusted him and he had failed. Rourk pushed his way through the spectators that had crowded around his best friend.

"Is he alive?" Rourk asked in a stiff voice. Blood was pooling around Tommy's head and dripping from his open mouth.

"He's still breathing, but he won't open his eyes or respond in any way. I saw it all. His head bounced pretty high off the ground." The man winced and looked back down at Tommy.

The driver paced nearby, his entire body shaking. He looked like he was just a kid. "He came out of nowhere."

Rourk glared at him, but didn't say anything.

"Where the hell is the ambulance?" Rourk snapped.

Just then, a dark-haired man in uniform ran forward, a medical bag in hand. "Out of the way, I'm a medic."

Rourk felt a spark of hope. Special Forces medics were highly trained. He would know what to do. Tommy was in better hands with him then an ambulance attendant. Rourk watched as he tore off Tommy's shirt. He cringed when he saw the blood.

Rourk's phone buzzed in his pocket. He closed his eyes and pulled it out. He really didn't want to talk to anyone. It was Thaddeus, so he snapped his phone open and walked away. "I was too late. It's bad."

"My mother is coming." Thaddeus's voice was subdued.

Rourk cleared his throat, pain in his chest. "Will he be ok?"

"I honestly don't know. It's not your fault,

Rourk. We don't have control over certain aspects of life."

"I should have been faster. Or talked to him longer this morning. He's like a brother to me."

"If he's still breathing when my mother gets there, he has a fighting chance."

"I have to go. I hear the sirens. Thank you for trying." Rourk clicked off the phone and shoved it in his pocket.

The ambulance pulled up and loaded Tommy onto the long flat board to immobilize his spine. *What if he was paralyzed?* Rourk thought, eyes widening. *Focus, Rourk...this is not helping anyone.*

Rourk strode up to the medic after the ambulance had pulled away. "What do you think?"

The man turned wary eyes to Rourk. He was a lean, fit man; his uniform was stained with Tommy's blood. He peeled off his blood-stained latex gloves as he said, "A friend of yours?"

"Yes."

The man took a deep breath, closing his eyes momentarily before answering. "I think it will be a miracle if he pulls through. The chance of internal injuries is too high. Who knows what that head injury did, or the state of his spinal cord. I'm sure it will be touch and go for awhile. I guess it depends on if it's his day to go or not."

Rourk grimaced. He knew the man spoke the truth. "Can you drop me off at the hospital?" he asked.

"Sure. My truck is over there." He pointed across the street to a large parking lot.

"Thank you." Rourk shifted his rucksack to the other shoulder and walked off with the man.

He wondered if Tommy could hold out until Emerald arrived.

They drove in silence. The medic pulled up to the emergency entrance to drop him off. "Sometimes it's better if they don't make it. I know that sounds harsh, but the things I've seen..."

Rourk nodded his head in agreement. He had also seen men walk away with injuries that made them wish they had died in battle. A car accident wasn't quite a battle, but brain injuries usually didn't end well. "Thanks for the ride." Rourk slammed the door shut.

The man waved and pulled out. Rourk took a deep breath and walked to the entrance.

"Rourk." The woman's urgent voice came from his right. He whirled to find Emerald striding towards him. "Do they have him?"

"Yeah. The ambulance left us behind, so they got here pretty quick."

She nodded. Her hair wasn't brushed; her short ginger locks were sticking up as if she'd just rolled from bed. Rourk figured she had— Thaddeus had likely woken her up and told her what was happening. Emerald probably took just long enough to get dressed before she teleported.

"I won't be able to get to him," she murmured, watching as an older couple shuffled by on their way into the building. She turned her bright blue eyes back to Rourk. "I'll have to find a quiet place. Go. Go in and check on him."

Rourk turned and she followed behind. The doors opened, admitting them into the cool interior. The smell of hospitals always bothered him a little. There was just something unnatural about it.

He stood impatiently in line to ask where they had sent Tommy. He stood rigid as he heard the people in front of them ask ridiculous questions: Where was the bathroom? How much longer do they have to wait? Can they make an appointment to come back later? Rourk tried to calm himself. Finally it was his turn. "My brother was hit by a vehicle and has been admitted. Can you tell me where he is?"

The woman behind the counter looked tired. Her mousey-brown hair was pulled into a bun that was falling apart, and there was a large coffee stain on her blue scrub shirt. She glanced at Rourk with non-sympathetic eyes. "Last name?"

"Sanders."

She tapped on her keyboard, the computer screen reflecting off her glasses. "He's in surgery."

Rourk's heart thudded. "Already?"

"Yes."

"Can you tell me what's wrong with him?"

She shook her head. "Confidential."

Rourk wanted to scream. Instead, he shoved his hand through his hair and took a calming breath. "What floor is he on?"

"Ninth floor."

"Thank you." Rourk and Emerald headed for the elevator. He wished Keegan was with him. He felt like he was about to unravel. He'd check on Tommy's status and then give her a call.

"I'm going to the restroom so I won't be disturbed. I'll find you when I'm done."

Rourk nodded and walked to the front desk. The nurse behind the counter smiled as he walked up. He leaned on his elbows atop the desk and said, "Can I have an update on my brother? Tommy Sanders?"

The woman stared at him for a moment. "That's funny. Your name-tag says Kavanagh."

Without missing a beat, Rourk said, "He's my stepbrother."

She nodded and pecked away at the keyboard. "He'll probably be in surgery a couple of hours. You're welcome to wait in the waiting area." She pointed to a small glass room to the left.

"Thanks. Can you let me know when they bring him out?"

"Yes, I'll have the doctor give you an update when they are done. Have you informed your parents?"

"Not yet. I was hoping to have some news before I freaked them out."

"Standard procedure. If he has them in his file, they will be notified."

Rourk nodded and moved to the waiting room. It was small and dimly lit. There was an old lady knitting in one corner as she watched the news; a stressed-looking young woman and a baby in another corner; and a middle-aged man who looked in serious need of sleep. Rourk couldn't help but notice how far they'd each sat away from each other, as if they were worried the other's bad luck would rub off.

Rourk slouched in a seat, dropped his head in his hands, and closed his eyes. He visualized Keegan. She was sitting in a classroom, her pen writing furiously on a notebook as she bit her tongue in concentration. He didn't want to bother her in class—he'd call her when he knew more.

It was only an hour before his phone buzzed. It was Tommy's mother. "Have you heard anything?" she asked anxiously.

"No, ma'am." Rourk looked around the room. The sun was high in the sky outside the one small window. The baby had finally gone to sleep.

"We're on our way. Our flight leaves at noon. Will you call me if you hear anything?" Her voice cracked over the sound of a loudspeaker in the background. They must have already been at the airport.

"Of course. Safe flight."

Two hours and thirteen minutes later, a man in scrubs walked into the room. Everyone stood wide-eyed as he entered. "Sanders?"

Rourk stood up and walked into the hall with the doctor, his palms clammy.

"I'm Doctor Wilson," the man said, offering his hand to Rourk. They shook.

"Your brother made it through the surgery," the doctor said. He was a tall man with large hands and creases on his face from the mask that hung around his neck. He rubbed his thumbs on his forehead. "Something odd happened. We went in to stop the internal bleeding, but once we got inside, we couldn't find anything. It just...vanished." The doctor shook his head. "I've never seen anything like it."

Rourk thought, *That's because you've never seen an elfin healer.* "Does that mean Tommy will be ok?"

"He's not out of the woods yet. We still have to worry about his brain. There's swelling. We need to wait and see if the swelling goes down on its own or if we have to make a hole to reduce the pressure." He paused and gestured for Rourk to have a seat in the uncomfortable metal chair outside the waiting room door. Doctor Wilson sat beside him, placing a hand on Rourk's arm. "There's also the matter of him regaining consciousness. In some cases, people never wake from comas."

"Thank you for being honest with me. When can I see him?"

"We're going to move him to ICU for observation. I'll have a nurse come get you when he can have visitors. Are his parents on the way?"

"Yes. They're coming from across the country, so they will be delayed."

The doctor clapped him on the shoulder one last time, and then left.

Rourk went back to the waiting area. He called Keegan—he needed to hear her voice. He filled her in on what had happened.

"Do you want me to come?" she asked softly, her voice soothing as it came over the line.

"No. We'll wait and see what happens. Your mom is here."

"Oh. Good." She was silent a moment. "I'd really rather come, Rourk."

"Stay in school, Keegan. I'll call you when I know more."

They talked for a few more minutes and said their goodbyes. Rourk stared at his phone and realized he felt much more centered after talking to his chosen.

Emerald breezed through the door into the waiting room and wrapped Rourk in a hug. When she pulled away, she held tightly to his shoulders and asked, "How's he doing?"

Rourk gave a half smile. "The doctors are baffled. They went into operate, and the internal bleeding had ceased on its own..."

"That's great news!" She stepped closer, looking around the room. She pushed both hands back through her hair, then smoothed it, before she said quietly, "I don't have as much control when I can't touch the person."

"They're worried about the brain swelling, and the fact that he hasn't responded."

Emerald sat heavily in a chair, leaning forward with her elbows on her knees. She looked tired. "I need to get in to see him."

"He's in the ICU so only immediate family members are allowed in. I'm still waiting for them to give me the go ahead to see him."

Emerald smiled. "Brother?"

"Yes."

"Alright, when they call you back just go along with what I say."

They waited and waited, flipping channels idly on the small, staticky television until a nurse finally came in and called Rourk back. Emerald stood up and followed him.

The nurse held up a hand to Emerald and shook her head. "Family members only."

"I'm a reiki master and also Tommy's godmother. His parents contacted me and wanted me to get in a soon as I could to give him a healing. It will only take 15-30 minutes. I know many hospitals now use reiki before and after surgeries." Emerald's tone was no-nonsense and held just a hint of command. Rourk was impressed.

The nurse thought about it for a moment. Rourk could almost see the wheels turning: It was still against policy, but her eyes held belief in the new age side of medicine. She shrugged and motioned for them to follow. "This way."

She led them to a service elevator at the end of the hallway, and pushed the button to go up. "When we get upstairs, you'll need to scrub your hands with sanitizer and we're going to give you face masks. We don't want anything brought into the room that could harm Tommy."

Rourk and Emerald both nodded, and Rourk answered, "Yes, ma'am. Absolutely."

The elevator was dimly lit by a single bulb. After the fluorescent lights of the waiting room and hallway, it was a welcome break on Rourk's eyes. They reached the 11th floor and the elevator dinged open.

After preparing to enter his room, Rourk and Emerald followed the nurse to an open, sliding-glass door marked by a number *10* and a clipboard with *T. Sanders* across the top.

"Twenty minutes," the nurse said softly.

"Thank you," Rourk and Emerald said in unison.

Tommy looked small and broken in the hospital bed. His body was stretched flat on his back and the bed was slightly raised so his head was higher than the rest. Several beeping machines were attached to him: one monitoring his heart rate which was slow and steady. There was a tube was coming out of his throat, and his eyes were closed.

Rourk took his hand, a lump in his throat. "You have to pull through Tommy. We're in this together."

Emerald moved to the other side of the bed and closed her eyes as she placed her hands lightly above the white gauze that covered Tommy's head.

Rourk watched Emerald curiously. A healer's magic was an incredible gift; they could heal almost anything, especially someone with the power of his chosen's mother. He knew if anyone could help Tommy it was her.

Emerald moved her hands around different areas of Tommy's head, her eyes closed. Her breathing was steady. She moved her hands down his chest—she would rest her hands in an area for a couple of minutes, then she would move to the next spot and repeat. She went over the rest of his body down to his feet, and then back to his head again.

The door opened and the nurse came in. "It's been twenty minutes. You can come back once they transfer him to the seventh floor."

Rourk was worried. He'd expected Tommy to wake up and be fine after the healing, but his eyes were still closed. Maybe it was his time.

As they walked towards the elevator, Emerald pulled Rourk into a half-hug. "I've done all I can, Rourk. I believe he will be fine, but we have to wait until he wakes up to be sure."

"I know." Rourk pushed the down button, then turned to face her. "I can't thank you enough."

The sound of the nurse's voice broke the silence of ICU as she called out the door of Tommy's room. "He's awake! Get the doctor."

Emerald smiled knowingly and patted

Rourk's arm. "I'm going to head back now. I left Warrick with Thaddeus. You know what a handful that little man is."

Rourk smiled. "Thank you, though I feel like that's not enough."

"It's more than enough. I'm glad I could help. That boy has a clear soul. The earth would be darker without people like him."

Rourk watched as Emerald stepped into the elevator. She waved, and the doors closed. Rourk knew she'd be gone before the elevator opened on the next floor. *So much power in such a little body.*

He called Keegan and gave her the good news. Rourk didn't need to hear from the doctors; he knew Tommy would be fine.

Thankfully, Tommy *was* fine. A week later, he was released from the hospital with nothing more than a few bumps and bruises, and the OK to return to work. There was no apparent brain damage, and his memories were still intact, as well as has reasoning skills. The doctors were shocked at his quick recovery.

Tommy kept telling everyone that a redheaded angel had saved him. Of course, the doctors wrote it off as a side-effect of his head injury. Rourk kept the truth to himself.

Chapter 13

Keegan's phone kept buzzing on her night stand.

She was so tired that she could barely keep her eyes open, but she rolled over and answered. "Hello."

"Keegan?"

She rubbed her eyes and looked at the clock: 3:33 in the morning. "Lauren, what's wrong?"

"I'm sorry to call so late. It's Donald. He's out of control."

Keegan's heart dropped, and she sat up in bed. Athena rolled over on her back and growled in her sleep. "What do you mean? Is he ok?"

"Ok, is a relative term. He's drinking all the time. I think he's even doing drugs. Plus, he's sleeping around with every girl he meets. And tonight he shifted into his tiger form on campus."

Keegan's hand flew to her cover her mouth. "Oh my god. Did anyone see him?"

"A couple of guys said they saw a tiger running around the campus. But everyone blew it off as they were drunk and didn't believe them. Thankfully, the campus is surrounded by woods so he wasn't visible for too long. The guys are at their wit's end with him. They don't know what to do. Calvron thought maybe if you came to talk to him it would help."

"He won't talk to me. I've sent him several texts and tried to call him, but he never responds."

"Do you think you could come here and try to talk to him in person? Keegan, this is bad. He can't be shifting in public."

Keegan sighed and rubbed a hand over her eyes. *First, Tommy, now Donald...* She pulled Athena close. "I don't know Lauren. I really don't think it would help, but I guess I can try. Anna was talking about coming to visit you soon. I will talk to her in the morning and find out when we can get a flight out."

"Thank you. I'm going to tell Calvron. I'll talk to you tomorrow."

"K. Bye." Keegan ended the call and sat back in her bed. She couldn't believe Donald was losing it like that. It wasn't like him. She knew he was upset, but she never knew him to lose control. He had always been the one to calm her when she was losing her temper. She really hoped she could do the same for him. But, she seriously doubted there was anything she could do. He couldn't stand her. She wrapped herself in the blankets and tried to fall back to sleep but spent the next three hours thinking about Donald.

When she saw it was a decent time, she picked up the phone and called Anna.

"Hey, do you want to go see Lauren in the

next day or so? She called me last night and told me Donald was out of control. He shifted on campus!"

"Are you serious? Yeah, I wanted to go see her soon anyway. I don't have classes tomorrow, and I can skip today. Want to see if we can get a flight out today?"

"Sure, I'll get online and see if I can get us tickets and call you back. Talk to you in a few minutes." Keegan ended the call and went straight to her computer. First, she got a flight to Seattle and then purchased tickets for both of them to California. Good thing for her dad's American Express, she thought wryly.

Keegan shrugged into a robe, then walked into the kitchen and turned on the coffee pot. She needed to let Rourk know, and she was worried he would be upset. She couldn't hide things from her chosen. Keegan closed her eyes to check on him. He was sitting in a small room surrounded by guys in uniforms. *Goodness, he looks hot in uniform.* Keegan grinned to herself. She watched as he looked up and tried to hide the smile forming on his lips. He knew she was thinking of him. She sent him a text that they needed to talk. She watched as he stood up and walked out of the room. A minute later, her phone rang.

"Rourk I have to tell you something that might not make you happy." Keegan paused as she sat on the couch and cradled a mug of coffee against her chest. Athena danced about on the rug in front of her, pulling a trail of toilet paper across the floor.

"You can tell me anything. Nothing will change the way I feel about you." Rourk tensed he had no idea what she was going to say and wasn't sure he wanted to hear it.

"I'm going to California today. Lauren called me and told me that Donald needs help. He has gotten out of control—he even shifted on campus. I'm not sure there is anything I can do to help him, but I need to try. He helped me so many times when I was about to lose my temper." Keegan paused briefly and hurried on. "You have nothing to worry about. I don't have feelings for him in that way anymore. I just want to try to help him as a friend. You are the only one for me."

She heard Rourk take a deep breath. "I trust you, Keegan. If you feel you need to do this, then I understand."

"You do?" She could hear the shock in her own voice.

"Yes, it's who you are. Your friends are important to you. I'm not going to say I am thrilled about the idea, but I will not try to stop you. How long do you think you will be there?"

"I'm not sure. Just a couple of days I think. I will be back before you come to visit. If anything keeps me there longer, you can meet me in California."

"Ok, keep me updated. Thank you for letting me know. I love you."

"I love you, too. You're the best! I'll text you and keep you in the loop. I can't wait to see you this weekend." Keegan smiled, hoping he could hear it in her voice.

"Me either. When are you leaving?"

"I'm flying out in three hours, and then I'll get a connecting plane with Anna this evening."

"What about Athena?" Rourk asked.

Keegan glanced down at the ball of white rubbing its back on the fluffy purple rug. The puppy jerked to a stop and panted, her dark eyes staring up at Keegan. "Oh. I don't know. I guess I could find a pet-sitter."

"Check the phone book for kennels. You can put her up for a few days."

Keegan nodded to herself. "Great idea."

"Ok, I have to get back into work," Rourk said. "I'll talk to you soon."

"Oh, one last thing." Keegan lowered her voice. "You are the sexiest man in that room."

Rourk laughed loudly. "Bye, Keegan."

Keegan disconnected and smiled as she refilled her coffee in the kitchen. She called Lauren and Anna to fill them in on plans before pulling out the phonebook to find a kennel. After the puppy situation was sorted, she packed her bags for the trip. She didn't bring much since she didn't plan to be there for long.

It was so good to see Anna. She had chopped her hair off: it was completely pink. Keegan hugged her tightly and didn't want to let go. "You look great. I love the hair. It looks so retro."

Anna fluffed up the side of her hair. "Thanks, I bleached it and it was driving me crazy so I went with pink. It was supposed to be red, but this is how it turned out." She shrugged.

"Well, it looks amazing. You look like a hip art student."

Anna was wearing skinny jeans and a long teal t-shirt with a belt cinched at her waist. Keegan definitely thought she looked like an art student; it was a look not many people could pull off, but Anna was stunning.

"You look fantastic too," Anna said, leaning over to hug Keegan again. Keegan had just thrown on a pair of holey jeans and a peasant top, going for comfort over style for the plane ride.

"Thanks."

"Let's go grab something to eat. There is an awesome bagel shop near by, and we can catch up." Anna laced her arm through Keegan's and led her to the parking lot.

They chatted about school on the drive to the bagel shop. Anna had made a lot of friends, and even gone on a few dates—which made Keegan feel like a failure. She still wasn't sure why she wasn't making a lot of friends in Alaska.

They walked into the bagel shop, and Keegan glanced around. It was a great atmosphere for hanging out: College students with laptops and books spread across their tables were sipping coffee and eating bagels. The walls were brown and hung with local art sporting reasonable price tags, and the large, dark mahogany counter was scarred by time. Keegan could see why Anna enjoyed hanging out there.

The girl at the cash register smiled. "Are you getting your regular today, Anna?"

Anna seemed to have found a place she fit in. Keegan was happy for her.

"Yep, that'd be great, Erica."

"What about your friend?" Erica turned her pale green eyes to Keegan.

"Um, do you have white chocolate mocha?"

"We sure do! What size?"

"Some things never change." Anna nudged Keegan with her elbow and smirked.

After they received their drinks, and Anna's bagel, they found a small table in the corner.

"We really need to get a place together. Living in a dorm sucks." Anna flung her bag over the back of her chair and fell into it. "My roommate is so annoying. Half the time, she shows up at three a.m. drunk or with some guy. Believe me, that is not something you want to wake up to."

Keegan shuddered. "Ugh. I would say not. Well, start looking for a place for us. I plan on moving here in January." She glanced around and motioned with her coffee cup. "This place looks much more happening than Alaska."

Anna's face lit up. "I'm so excited! I've really missed having you around."

"So, what has been going on with you? Are you dating anyone?" Keegan raised an eyebrow and took a sip of her coffee.

"Keegan, there are so many hot guys here it is insane! I just want to gobble them all up." She tilted her head towards a guy across the room.

Keegan glanced over, trying to be surreptitious. He was indeed nice eye candy. "Can't you cast a spell on him or something?"

"Why yes, actually I can. However, I want someone to like me for *me*, not for a spell. I'm not opposed to using one if I get too desperate though." Anna winked.

Keegan laughed. "I've really missed this."

Anna leaned forward and lowered her voice. Her sparkly blue eye shadow glinted in the low light hanging over their table. "So Donald really shifted in public? You must have done a number on that poor boy."

"I feel horrible. Hopefully, we can talk some

sense into him."

They sat and chatted for a couple of hours before they went to Anna's dorm room and picked up her bag; they had a flight to catch and a tiger to save.

Lauren, Spencer, Sam, and Calvron greeted them at the airport. They all looked older and more mature; it made Keegan kinda sad. She missed the days of them chasing each other around school like children, getting yelled at by teachers to slow down and grow up.

Calvron's style had changed significantly. He was at one point as outrageous as Anna had been, but was more subdued now. He was wearing a pair of dark jeans and a plain red t-shirt. His messy blonde hair hadn't changed.

Lauren pulled the girls into a hug. She hadn't really changed: her dark hair was still long and curly and pulled back into a low ponytail. The pink sundress she wore showed off her toned arms and legs. Lauren was one of the most beautiful girls Keegan knew.

It hadn't been that long since they had seen each other, but it felt like a lifetime. They were growing apart, and they all knew it. It was hard to let go of childhood.

Calvron cleared his throat. "We have a serious problem and even I am at a loss of what to do."

Keegan was flooded by guilt. She knew she was the cause of the whole mess.

"Can't you use magic to rein him in?" Keegan asked.

"I've been trying, and it has been helping

somewhat, but not nearly enough. I think he has to hit rock bottom before we can help him. I thought maybe if we staged a sort of intervention, we might be able to get through to him." Calvron met Keegan's eyes. "I hope you can get through to him."

Keegan shook her head. "I can try. Just don't be surprised if he wants nothing to do with me."

"Where is he now?" Anna wondered aloud.

"We have no idea," Sam answered with a shrug. "He's been gone for days, and we can't find him anywhere."

Anna spoke up. "I can find him. I'll put a tracking spell on him."

They all looked at Anna in surprise.

"Obviously you've been working on your skills." Calvron sounded pleased. Keegan noticed the way he appraised Anna, as if he were seeing her in a new light.

"Yes," Anna answered, blushing. "I've found a couple of solitary witches in Seattle. We meet up once a week for ritual and discussion. I've learned so much."

"Let's get out of here." Spencer grabbed Keegan's bag and carried it for her as they headed for the door. He was tall, with black hair and vivid green eyes. He bumped gently against Keegan and whispered, "It's not your fault."

She sighed. "I feel like it is. It makes me so sad."

Blond-haired, blue-eyed Sam overheard and butted in. "You should feel bad. You shattered the poor guy's heart."

Calvron stopped walking and turned towards them, eyeing Sam sternly. "No one is to blame. It is what it is. We live in a world of magic. We have to accept that we don't always have control of our life path. That's something Donald needs to learn."

This declaration quieted them all as they got Anna's and Keegan's luggage and walked out the door.

Lauren spoke up as they reached her car in the parking garage. "We'll go to my place. It's big, and I don't have a roommate. Anna, do we need to stop and get anything for the spell?"

Anna shook her head no. "I have everything I need."

Lauren's apartment was in an old converted warehouse in an artsy district of the city. It didn't look like much on the outside—just a big, concrete square—but inside, it was lofty and spacious.

"It's mostly students," she told Keegan as she locked the door behind them. "My neighbors are all really cool. There are parties almost every weekend somewhere in the building."

"This is gorgeous," Keegan said, and sighed as she thought of her tiny apartment in Alaska. The ceilings were high, with exposed ductwork and track lighting. One wall was nothing but windows that looked out over a busy street. The floor plan was open—the kitchen counter overlooked a centrally placed living room with a matching black leather couch set and television.

"You guys can stay in here," Lauren said, opening a closed door down a small hallway. "It's my only spare room, just the one bed but it's king-sized. Do you mind?"

"Nope," Anna said and flopped on the black comforter.

Keegan laughed, dropping her bags against the dresser. "I can't believe how nice this place is."

"Yeah. My parents are paying for it, just as long as I keep my grades up." Lauren touched the doorframe. "I really didn't want to live in a dorm."

"No, you really don't!" Anna called, her voice muffled from the blanket.

"Her roommate is a drunk," Keegan clarified, and Lauren nodded sagely.

"My bedroom is across the hall, and the bathroom is right next door. Do you guys need anything right now?"

"Something to drink would be great," Keegan answered as she realized she was thirsty.

Lauren nodded. "I got juice and stuff." She glanced over at Anna. "Are you going to get ready to do the ritual?"

"Yeah. I'll meet you guys out there in two minutes."

Anna hadn't brought her robe from home, so she felt a little naked as she set the living room for the ritual. She made do with a pair of sweatpants and a t-shirt made of cotton—natural materials that wouldn't stunt the use of her magic.

"Lauren, can you turn the lights down?" she asked when she was done arranging her tools.

Lauren nodded and killed the lights. The wall of windows let in just enough of the slowly disappearing daylight.

Anna took a deep breath, standing before the coffee table—her impromptu altar. "I need complete silence for this to work."

She walked around with her pocket compass to locate North, where she placed a bowl of salt. To the East, a burning stick of Sandlewood incense. At the South, Anna set a white votive candle, and to the West, a small cup of water. She took out a photo of Donald and placed it on the altar, along with a black onyx crystal. She knelt down before the table, closed her eyes, and began to chant.

> *Keeper of Donald, hear me now...open your ears.*
> *Find for me where we need to be*
> *By moon, sun, earth, air, fire and sea.*
> *Someone I lost I need to find,*
> *By the power of three this spell I bind.*

Anna said the chant three times. When she was done, she focused on the energy that surrounded her and concentrated on Donald with her eyes tightly shut. At first, she saw nothing but the darkness of her eyelids and was worried the spell wouldn't work.

Take deep breaths, she heard the voice of her old teacher, Magdalena, echo in her mind. Anna relaxed and pictured Donald's face: his bright blue eyes and crooked smile. The haze started to fade away. A tiger formed in her mind's eye; he was laying on a patch of pillowy grass in a forest. He looked around, as if he knew someone was there. The tiger yawned and stretched to a standing position, and then took off in a sprint.

Anna followed him through the woods, her astral body easily keeping up. When he shifted to his human form, Anna had to suppress a laugh—he was naked. She could see why Keegan had been attracted to him. She watched his muscular frame as he walked behind a tree and grabbed a bag he had obviously placed there earlier. He walked back out in jeans and a flannel shirt. With his hands shoved deep in his pockets and his orange hair reflecting the evening sun, Donald walked over a hill and down into a clearing with Anna on his tail.

Before long, Anna saw a sign that said Arcata.

The room was eerily silent as Anna's eyes opened. She sat stoically, watching the candle melt till nothing was left. She felt Lauren and Keegan's eyes on her. Finally, she rose to her feet. "I know where he is."

"Where?" Keegan asked.

Anna looked over her shoulder. Her friends were nearly invisible—it had gotten dark since she started the ritual. "Arcata. It's beautiful there."

Lauren looked puzzled. "That's over four hours away by car."

Anna shrugged. "All I know is that's where he is, and he's walking through town now."

"I'll call Calvron and tell him," Lauren said, pulling out her cell phone.

Keegan pushed herself from the floor and dusted off her hands. "I hope this works."

The girls climbed into Lauren's silver Prius and started the four-hour journey in search of Donald. Calvron and the guys would be meeting them in Arcata.

Keegan turned sideways to look at Lauren.

"So, tell us. Are you seeing anyone?"

Lauren grinned slyly. "Actually, I recently met a guy. He is the hottest guy I've ever laid eyes on." She paused dramatically. "And he's a dark fairy."

Keegan and Anna's eyes widened in surprise. Anna gasped, "A dark fairy? Is that even allowed?"

Lauren shrugged. "I've never heard of it before. I Googled it, but you know what info on the internet is like."

"Yeah. Elves live at the North Pole with Santa," Keegan said wryly.

"Exactly." Lauren shrugged. "From what I can tell, it's kinda like the dark and light elves, Keegan. Not so much an 'evil' thing, just...*different*."

"I know what you mean," Keegan responded, touching Lauren's arm. "My dad is friends with the leader of the dark elves now. It's still weird."

Lauren nodded. "Yeah, that is weird. Anyway, I just can't resist him. Grab my phone and open the pictures, you'll see him."

Anna reached forward and grabbed Lauren's phone from the center console. She pecked at the screen, opening up the images, and said, "Wow! He is hot! I guess I can't blame you."

Keegan turned towards the back and reached for the phone. "Hotter than Rourk?"

Anna looked back down at the photo. "Much hotter."

"Let me see that." Keegan grabbed the phone from Anna. She stared down into the face of a striking young man. He had olive skin, high cheek bones, a perfect nose, and the palest green eyes she had ever seen on a person. He was beautiful.

"He doesn't look evil."

Lauren grabbed the phone from her and glanced down quickly to smile at the picture. She turned her eyes back to the road. "He isn't evil," she said indignantly. "Tristen is the most thoughtful, intelligent man I have ever met. You'll see when you meet him."

Chapter 14

They reached Arcata before night fell completely.

The town was not a large one, so they drove around in hopes of spotting Donald—with no luck. Old-fashioned mom-and-pop stores lined the streets. There was a good crowd on the sidewalks: couples out for evening strolls and smiling shoppers walking in and out of the stores.

Calvron called Keegan's cell after about an hour. "Anything?"

"No, nothing," Keegan said, dejected.

"Figures." He sighed through the phone line. "Alright, well, we're hungry. You want to take a break for dinner?"

"Sounds good."

"There's a great place called Bertha's— Lauren knows it. We'll meet you there."

"The guys wanna eat. Bertha's?"

"Yeah, it's their favorite," Lauren answered, making a U-turn and heading back in the other direction.

A loud bell chimed as they walked through the door at the diner, startling Keegan. She was on edge because of Donald, but she hadn't realized how famished she was. It had been a long time since she and Anna had eaten lunch at the airport. The smell of pot roast made her stomach growl.

Calvron asked the employees if anyone had seen an orange-haired guy lately. One of the waitress said she saw him earlier that day, walking down the street.

"I stopped and asked if he wanted a ride and he refused." She shrugged her shoulders and went on to the next table.

After dinner, they ended up getting a couple of rooms at a small hotel, deciding they would start the search fresh in the morning. The room smelled clean, and the bed looked soft and inviting. The girls dropped their bags on the ground. Keegan threw herself on the bed, Anna went to the bathroom, and Lauren pulled out her phone to text her boyfriend.

Her legs crossed at the ankles and her hands behind her head, Keegan stared at the ceiling and thought of Donald. She hoped they found him soon; in two days Rourk was supposed to be visiting her in Alaska.

Keegan ran her fingers over the stones on her necklace and smiled. She had grown attached to the ugly necklace because it reminded her of her bond with Rourk. She loved knowing that he knew when she was thinking of him. They had texted back and forth a few times while she was searching earlier, and she was anxious to see him on Friday. She also checked on him throughout the day with her mind's eye; she couldn't seem to stop herself. She was addicted to him.

Keegan woke up to the sound of Lauren and Anna laughing. They were already up and dressed. Sometimes, she really wished she were a morning person.

"I need coffee," Keegan groaned from the bed.

Her friends turned and looked at her.

"It's about time," Anna teased with one eyebrow raised.

"We've been waiting for hours for you to wake up," Lauren said.

Keegan threw the blankets to the side and swung her feet to the ground. Rubbing her eyes, she walked to the bathroom. "I'll be ready soon. Can someone get me some coffee?"

The girls glanced at each other and Lauren said, "Sure. There's a coffee shop down the street. We'll be back in a bit."

When Lauren and Anna walked through the door of the coffee shop, they found Donald sitting at a table in the corner. His bright orange hair would stand out anywhere. He looked up when he heard the bell chime; his body stiffened when he saw them.

Lauren slid into the booth and Anna followed. They stared across at him, not sure what to say.

"What are you doing here?" Donald said gruffly.

"We're here to help you." Lauren reached over to grab his hand.

"I don't need any help." He pulled his hand back.

"Keegan is here." Anna said softly.

Pain flashed across his face. He turned away, his eyes studying the people hurrying past outside the window "Why?"

"She said you haven't returned her calls or texts, so she was worried about you," Lauren said quietly.

"Where is she?"

"She's back at the hotel. She slept in so she sent us for coffee."

The corner of his mouth quirked up as if he were going to smile and stopped himself. "Tell her to go home. I don't want to see her, and I don't need your help." He stood up, threw a $20 bill on the table, and walked out.

"Well that went well." Anna reached over and grabbed a slice of toast from his plate while Lauren rolled her eyes.

They ordered their coffees and went back to the hotel. The guys were already waiting in the lobby, so they filled them in on the exchange.

Calvron narrowed his eyes and tapped a finger on his chin. "I could probably track him if he changed into his tiger form."

Spencer and Sam exchanged looks, and the three guys bolted out of the hotel, hoping to catch Donald before he got too far.

Anna handed Keegan her coffee as she came out of the bathroom still wrapped in a towel.

"We saw Donald at the coffee shop," she said with a frown.

Keegan stopped, clutching the towel at her chest. "What?"

"Yeah. He was sitting inside. We talked to

him."

"I'm sorry Keegan, but I really think he doesn't want to see you," Lauren cut in as she sat on the bed.

"I didn't think he would." Proof that he didn't filled her with sadness. She hated that she had caused his unhappiness. "But, Calvron asked me to try, so I have to."

Calvron, Spencer, and Sam showed up a couple of hours later and knocked on the girls' door.

"Hey," Keegan said when she opened it. "Did you find him?"

Spencer shook his head. "No. He's gone."

"Again," Calvron said disgustedly.

Anna grabbed her bag and started setting up her altar. "If you guys can step out really quick, I'll track him."

Keegan watched in awe as Anna's movements were sure and quick. She had turned into a completely different person. Gone was the quirky, awkward girl Keegan had grown up with. She had been replaced by a beautiful, confident—and powerful—witch.

Anna eventually turned towards them and motioned for Keegan to let the guys back in. "Maybe we should just leave him alone. He really doesn't want to be found, and I don't think he's ready for our help."

Calvron stepped towards her. "What did you see? Where is he?'

"He's not far from here. He's in the woods. Watching us." Anna sighed and began to put away her crystals.

Keegan looked up from the bed. "He's close?"

"Yes. He's behind the hotel in the woods." Anna started picking up her things. She held onto her crystal for a few minutes and closed her eyes, smiling.

"I think I should go talk to him by myself." Keegan walked over and grabbed her coat. She needed to at least *try* to speak to him. Alone.

Sam spoke up. "I don't think that is a great idea. We should all go together. He's made it obvious he doesn't want to see you. You'll probably make him run."

Keegan zipped her jacket. "I'm going. Don't follow me." She walked out the door and didn't look back.

The woods weren't that far away. She thought about Donald as she walked, and all the good times they had shared together. He was her rock when she was dealing with her emotions of coming back to life from the black magic. She wasn't sure what would have happened to her had it not been for him. Every time the darkness came to her, he had been there to push it back. She owed him.

She walked into the woods and looked around at the huge trees. She knew he would know she was there if he was in his tiger form. She walked deeper into the woods and tried to be as loud as possible, stomping on fallen branches so that they cracked under her feet. "Donald, please come talk to me. I know you're here."

Rocks fell from above, startling Keegan; she looked up and saw it was Donald. He was standing on the edge of an embankment not too far from her, watching her. He looked different. He was scruffy with a few days' growth on his face, and his hair was crazier than usual. She smiled when she noticed his shirt was buttoned wrong.

The hill wasn't that high so she started to climb up. Donald didn't move; he just watched her. She'd almost made it to the top when she slipped on the loose rocks and started sliding back down. He ran towards her and offered his hand.

Keegan grasped his hand. Donald grabbed her forearm and pulled her up. His hand was so warm against her skin. She stared into his startling blue eyes. "Thank you."

Donald returned her stare, but didn't say anything. He dropped her hand and shoved his own hands in his pockets.

Keegan thought carefully before she spoke. She didn't want to make it any worse.

He looked so much older than the last time she saw him. She knew she would only have one shot at getting through to him. "It seems the tables have turned. What's going on with you Donald? I'm not worth this. You deserve so much more."

"You're worth it to me." Donald kicked at the ground, refusing to meet her eyes.

"I'm sorry I hurt you. You have to know that was never my intention."

"I'm not mad at you, Keegan. I know it's not your fault." He looked off in the distance. "I just can't seem to accept that you're gone. You're everything to me."

Keegan didn't know what to say to that. Her heart ached for him.

"Are you happy?" Donald asked. Keegan could hear the pain in his voice.

"Yes." She took a step towards him. "But I'm not happy that you're going through this."

"Can't you try to fight the bond Keegan? We were great together."

"I couldn't if I wanted to," she said softly.

"Why are you even here? Why don't you go back to your chosen?" Donald glared at her.

"Magic is beyond us, Donald. We just have to accept it. You *will* find someone new and forget all about me."

"I don't want anyone else."

Donald reached for her, both of his hands grasping her arms. He pulled her against him and tried to kiss her.

"Donald!" Keegan pushed him roughly away. "I can't."

"You had no problem kissing him when we were together," Donald spat, his hands balling into fists at his sides.

Keegan stared at him, wondering if the Donald she knew was still inside him.

"I want you to see something. I want you to see the strength of an elf's bond." Keegan reached up and unclasped her necklace, letting it drop to the ground.

Pain flashed in her eyes as she clutched her stomach and doubled over. The pain hit her with an intensity she hadn't expected; she couldn't breathe.

"What's wrong?" Donald bent down and tried to hold her up, but she fell to the ground and curled up as the pain coursed through her body.

Donald was frantic. "Keegan, please, what's going on? Tell me how to fix it."

"Necklace." She managed to get out between

clenched teeth.

Donald looked around in a panic and found the necklace of pink stones laying on the ground. He grabbed it with shaking hands and tried to clasp it around Keegan's neck.

Slowly, the pain dissipated from her body, allowing her body to relax. She stayed on the ground, waiting for it to disappear entirely.

Donald was on his knees beside her, his breath coming fast. He wrapped his arms around her, holding her tightly. "Keegan, what just happened? Are you ok?"

Keegan pulled herself up to sitting position and tried not to think about the lingering pain. "When I'm separated from Rourk, that is what happens to my body. My mom made a necklace to keep the worst of it at bay."

Donald stared at her, the disbelief clear on his face. "He did that to you? I'll kill him."

She had never heard the edge in his voice before. "He didn't do it. The bond did. I told you— we can't fight the bond. Would you want me to be in constant pain?"

Donald looked away, his jaw clenched. "Are you only with him to avoid pain?"

Keegan smiled sadly. "No, my heart needs him Donald. I can't be with anyone except him. We are made for each other, and I love him."

"If you came here to make me feel better, you didn't do a very good job. You need to leave." He stood up and put distance between them.

"Please, don't shut me out. I still want to be your friend."

Donald laughed. "Not going to happen." He shifted and took off into the woods.

Keegan reached down and picked up his clothing. Her heart ached—she really thought she would be able to get through to him. It seemed she might have made things worse.

Back at the hotel, she told everyone what happened, then called Rourk and filled him in.

"So am I coming to Alaska or California tomorrow? I need to get my ticket," Rourk said calmly.

"I don't know what to do. I don't think I can help him. I don't think anyone can help him until he is ready. They want to stay the weekend and see if the guys can get through to him. I don't know if I should stay or just go home. Anna and Lauren are staying."

"I'll make my ticket to California. I know you want to be there. I really don't care where I go as long as I'm with you."

"Thank you. I can't wait to see you."

"Keegan, please don't take off your necklace again until I'm around. I really hate knowing you were in pain."

"I won't. I promise. I really thought it would help."

Chapter 15

During the flight, Rourk thought about the shifter, and tried to see things from his point of view. Rourk knew what it felt like to lose Keegan, and it wasn't a good feeling.

However, the boy should simply have more self control than he'd been showing. Rourk was slightly disgusted with the fact that he shifted in public; it was really inexcusable.

Because of the time difference, his flight touched down in California fairly early. His pulse quickened as he walked off the plane. Just the thought of seeing Keegan drove him crazy. He had to consciously tell himself not to push people out of the way to get to her. Through the sea of people, all he saw was her beautiful smile. He loved the way her eyes lit up when she saw him. He lengthened his stride and pulled her into his arms, inhaling the scent of sandalwood and vanilla. "I've missed you."

"You better." Keegan grinned. "I'm so glad

you're here. I felt lost without you."

Rourk ran his hands through her hair and she tilted her head to meet his lips. It was as if all the people in the airport disappeared and it was only them. He loved the way she made him feel.

Rourk took a step back to take her in. He smiled when he saw the blush creep up her face. "How are you doing?"

"I'm fine, much better now that you're here. Thank you for coming." She gave him a slight smile. "I'm sure it's not easy for you."

Rourk laughed. "It's fine Keegan. As long as I am with you I really don't care where we are." He laced his fingers between hers and walked out towards the exit. "I get to properly meet your friends."

Keegan squeezed his hand. "Don't expect a warm welcome from the guys, but Anna and Lauren will be excited to meet you. I got you a room next to ours. I hope that is ok?"

"Thank you. So, no luck talking sense into Donald?"

"He wouldn't listen to me. I think he hates me."

Rourk shook his head. "He doesn't hate you. If he hated you, he wouldn't be taking things so hard. I'm sure he wishes he could hate you. It would make his life easier."

Keegan tilted her head to the side and looked up at him, her blue-green eyes looked serious. "Did you wish you could hate me?"

"No, I didn't bother to try to fight my feelings for you. I knew it would be useless." Rourk wrapped his arm around her and pulled her closer. "We're together now. I don't like to dwell on the past."

Keegan knocked on the door and Lauren flung it open. "It's about time. Rourk, it's so good to finally meet you. I don't think we got introduced at Keegan's birthday party." Lauren winked and nudged his arm.

"Keegan talks about you two constantly. She is lucky to have such great friends." Rourk smiled over at Anna, and she waved back.

"Are you starving? There's a little diner down the street. Actually, my stomach just growled. We're going to eat." Anna stood up and moved towards the door.

Keegan looked over at Rourk and he shrugged. "That works for me. Let me just throw my bag in my room and I'll be right back."

Keegan grinned at the girls after he left the room. "Isn't he amazing?"

Lauren gave a mischievous grin. "Spill the beans. How's the elven sex? I imagine with his intensity it's incredible."

Keegan looked down at the tan worn carpet and focused on a spot on the floor. "I wouldn't know. He wants to wait till we get married."

"Get out of here!" Anna pushed her and almost made her fall to the ground. "That boy is too good to be true."

Anna sighed. "How is it possible that the three of us are still virgins? We're hot right?"

Keegan laughed, and Lauren was strangely quiet.

"Lauren!" The both said at the same time.

Anna screamed, "You lost your virginity and didn't tell us?"

Lauren had a far away look on her face with a secret smile. "I told you about Tristen."

"We want details. Is it wonderful?" Anna asked.

"You have no idea. I can't even begin to describe it. It's like we're brought to another dimension. I know that sounds ridiculous, and I'm sure it's because we are both fairies, although I have nothing to compare it to." Her face flushed red.

A knock on the door startled them out of their thoughts.

Keegan opened the door. Rourk stood on the other side, running his hands through his hair. "Am I interrupting something?"

"Nope, just girl talk. Let's go eat." Keegan put her arm through his and they left for dinner.

Lauren had invited the guys, but Keegan guessed they decided not to show up. Which was understandable, but the girls found it slightly annoying. It wasn't as if Rourk had any control over being Keegan's chosen.

Keegan enjoyed seeing her friends get to know Rourk better, although he seemed uncomfortable being grilled by them.

"When are you moving to Washington?" Anna asked.

"If everything goes as planned we should be moving next month."

Keegan's eyes lit up. "Really?"

Rourk put his hand on hers. "Really. Tommy has already been looking for a place for us."

"Ohhh...who is Tommy? Is he hot like you?" Ann grinned wickedly and rubbed her hands together.

Rourk's face flushed, and he looked at Keegan for help. "He's a friend I made at basic training, and we'll be roommates. He's a great guy."

Anna slumped in her seat. "Great guy is codeword for not a sexy beast."

They all laughed.

"Keegan, you'll be moving soon too, right?" Lauren reached over and grabbed a napkin.

"Yep. I'm going to move in with Anna—well, we're going to get a place together."

"I'm so jealous." Lauren sighed. "Tristen and I will have to come visit once you guys get settled in."

"Sounds pretty serious." Keegan raised an eyebrow.

Lauren smiled. "I hope it is. We haven't been together long, but I know he's the one."

"I don't think I'll ever find anyone." Anna frowned.

Keegan decided to change the subject. "So what are we going to do about Donald? I have to leave by Sunday."

"I don't know, maybe we should just leave him alone. I wouldn't want someone chasing after me if I wanted to be alone," Lauren said.

"Does anyone know if he has shifted in public again or if it was a one-time occurrence? That's the main issue. Can you imagine if the humans realized shifters were real? That would be trouble for all of us." Rourk glanced around at the girls seriously before he took a bite out of his sandwich.

"I've only heard of the one incidence, but who knows? There could have been more. He gets drunk all the time and loses control. I don't think he has been to a class in weeks," Lauren said.

Keegan lowered her head. "It's all my fault. I should have handled things differently."

"It's not your fault, Keegan. You have no control of how someone reacts." Rourk squeezed her hand under the table.

They spent the day driving around and looking for Donald. Occasionally, they stopped to ask passers-by if anyone had spotted him, but no one had. He was probably hiding in the woods, or he had moved on. After a day of no luck, they all went to their rooms for the night and agreed to try again tomorrow. If they didn't have any luck, Anna would use a spell to track his location again.

Rourk had an idea of his own, but he didn't want to let the girls in on the plan. Tracking was what he did best. He knew as long as Donald was in the area, he could find him. Usually, Rourk would take the hard route and search for him without using his powers, but they were running short on time. He wanted to get this wrapped up so he could spend more time with Keegan.

He shook his head at the simplicity of it all, closed his eyes, and thought of nothing else but Donald. Rourk saw the dimly lit room with a tacky neon sign the said "Beer Here." He tried to look around for clues, but his gift only allowed him to see the person he was thinking of and whatever was directly behind that person. Donald was sitting at a bar drinking and looking pissed off. Rourk snapped his eyes open.

He grabbed his laptop; he was surprised how much it had come in handy. Rourk searched for local bars: there were five. He would check them systematically. He wasn't sure what he would say to the shifter, but he was hoping he could talk some sense into him. Rourk grabbed his jacket and headed out on foot.

The town was quiet as he walked the streets one by one, going into the bars, and not seeing Donald. When he made it to the third rundown bar, he heard raised voices and thought his luck had changed. No one noticed Rourk when he walked in. They were too focused on the commotion in the corner.

The bar was dark and smelled of cigarettes and cheap perfume. Three guys had Donald backed into a corner. His eyes were wild, liked a caged animal, and Rourk knew his instinct was to shift. Rourk couldn't allow that to happen.

A hush fell over the patrons as Rourk walked confidently up to the three men. A man with a goatee had a beer bottle with broken, jagged edges and was holding it by the stem.

"Leave him alone," Rourk called out evenly.

"Oh yeah? And what are you going to do about it?" A bald guy with bulging muscles glanced over at Rourk with a laugh.

"Let's just say it won't be pretty. Let him go now and you guys can all walk away unharmed."

"Get out of here, Rourk. I don't need your help," Donald spat.

"I told you to keep your mouth shut, punk." The guy holding Donald against the wall punched him in the face.

Donald wiped the blood from his mouth and glared at Rourk.

Rourk said nothing. He watched the largest man with tribal tattoos walk towards him.

"Oh so you think you're a tough guy, huh?"

He must have been at least 6'2" and over 200 pounds. He had on a worn leather jacket. He looked like he had been in his share of fights in his day. His nose was crooked from being broken too many times. As soon as he was in striking distance, Rourk sprung. He knew better than to hesitate. The large man threw a punch, which Rourk blocked easily. Rourk slammed his head into the guy's nose and blood poured out. The man seemed dazed and started to fall forward. Rourk swiftly turned the man to face his buddies. Rourk had the guy's elbow pressed against his own back. He groaned.

"Let my friend go," Rourk said calmly.

"I'm not your friend." Donald glared at Rourk.

The two men that had Donald looked at each other and the one with the broken bottle dropped his grip on Donald and moved forward. Rourk kneed the bald one hard in the back and as he dropped to his knees, Rourk slammed his elbow into the guy's temple. The man dropped to the ground. Rourk then went after the other man, who was still advancing towards him.

He had a crazed look in his eyes as he rushed forward, ready to strike. Rourk sidestepped and raised his arm to block the glass and rammed his other hand into the man's throat, crushing his windpipe. The guy's brown eyes widened as he dropped the glass, and his hands flew to his throat.

The last man standing fidgeted nervously. He was much smaller than the others. He pushed Donald towards Rourk. "You can have him. Just make sure he never comes back to this bar again."

Rourk nodded at the man and grabbed Donald's arm to lead him out.

Donald yanked his arm away. "Don't touch me."

"You're welcome."

"I didn't ask for your help. Why are you even here?" His words slurred slightly from too much drink.

"I know what you are going through. Trust me. It's not too long ago that you took Keegan from me. Not that I blame you, I would have done the same thing."

Donald stopped walking and stared at Rourk. "You have no idea what I am going through. I feel empty. I just want to feel again. When I was with Keegan..."

"Let her go. She is not coming back and you know it."

"What do you think I have been trying to do?" Donald hung his head.

"Shifting in public is trying to let go? You are putting everyone in danger with your recklessness. I would expect more from someone who had earned Keegan's affection. You can't fight magic, shifter. If Keegan had chosen you over me, I would have walked away and let her be happy. If you cared for her half as much as you claim, you will do the same." Rourk turned and walked away.

Chapter 16

Keegan woke up to the ding of her phone. She wiped the sleep from her eyes and was surprised to see it was from Donald.

I'm sorry for being such an ass. I need to go away for awhile and get myself straight. Tell the guys I'll be back next semester. You deserve to be happy. Rourk is a lucky man.

Keegan fumbled to reply. *Are you ok? Do you want to meet?*

I'm long gone. Don't worry about me, I'll be fine. Someone talked some sense into me.

I'm glad you are ok. I'm sorry I hurt you.

Not your fault. Take care, and thank you for the time we had together.

Keegan wiped a tear from her cheek. *We had fun. You'll always be special to me.*

But I'll never be your chosen.

No, I'm sorry he was picked for me long before we met.

I know. Bye Keegan.

Stay safe. Keegan sat up in bed and stared at the phone. She truly hoped he was ok. She wished she could tell him what Thaddeus had told her about the white tiger, but she knew that would be crossing the line. He had to find her on his own. Let life take the course it was meant to take.

Anna and Lauren were stirring. Once they were awake, Keegan filled them in on the texts.

"I wonder what changed his mind?" Anna murmured, stretching under the covers.

"I don't know. He didn't say."

"There's nothing else we can do," Lauren said. She was lying on her stomach, hugging her pillow with both arms.

Anna smiled. "I guess it's time to go home, then. Our job is done."

Keegan decided she would just stay there with Rourk since he only had one more day. There was no sense in having him pay for another plane ticket. Anna and Lauren packed their things and said their goodbyes, followed by Spencer, Sam and Calvron, who were angry Donald hadn't contacted them.

Keegan got dressed and knocked on Rourk's door. He opened it with a welcoming smile.

"Wasn't sure you were ever going to show up." He wrapped his arms around her waist and pulled her in.

"Just had to say goodbye to everyone. It's just me and you left." She bit her lip and smiled up at him.

"You have no idea how happy that makes me." Rourk's grey eyes twinkled in the sunlight.

"Donald texted me that he had to get away to get himself right again."

"That's good." Rourk's expression didn't change.

"He said someone talked some sense into him. Do you happen to know who that was?"

"We might have had words." Rourk stared down at her, his face stoic.

"Whatever you said seems to have helped. He said you were lucky."

"I am lucky." Rourk tucked a finger under her chin and tilted her head up for a kiss.

Keegan loved the feel of his lips on hers. He tangled his hands in her hair, intensifying the kiss until she was breathless. She always got so caught up in their kisses.

Grudgingly, she pulled back, and stared into his grey eyes that she loved so much. "So, what do you want to do today? And please don't say hiking."

Rourk laughed loudly. "Ok, well, that was my first thought. There are tons of trails around here. What would you like to do? Shop, play tourist, or just hang out in the room?"

"As much as hanging out in the room sounds appealing, I think I would want to attack you. We should probably play tourist. I've never been to California before. This town looks pretty neat; we can go explore. If there is nothing of interest, we can always take a long drive to the next city." Keegan ran her fingers up his arm. It made her fingertips tingle.

"Rourk, I want to get married," Keegan blurted, and then blushed.

He took a step back, his hands on the side of

her arms as he looked at her closely. "Where is this coming from?"

"I want to be with you always. It's killing me being separated from you."

"You will always be with me, and we would be separated regardless because of the military. I will soon be in Washington with you."

"I know but I want to wake up with you every morning, and greet you when you get home from work."

"Does this have anything to do with Donald? I don't get the sudden change. You know I would marry you today, but I need to be sure this is what you really want and not some whim."

"Well, it does kinda have something to do with Donald." She felt Rourk's body tense up.

"Not in a bad way. You're the only one for me. We're meant to be together. I've just been stubborn. I don't even know why I tried to go against tradition. It was just sprung on me so quickly." She gazed into his eyes. "I want to be your wife. I want to grow old with you and someday have little elf babies running around."

Rourk grinned widely. "You have made me the happiest man in the world."

"That's a little dramatic. But I like the sound of it." Keegan leaned up and Rourk kissed her.

"So how soon are you thinking? We could fly out to Vegas tonight." Rourk raised an eyebrow and grinned.

"It's fall and I've always wanted a fall wedding. I really want to get married on the property at my favorite spot. My mom is going to freak out." Keegan was starting to get excited about planning the handfasting. Her mind raced with all the things they would have to do. Elves tended to have large weddings. Any excuse to throw a party was a good one.

"I love the idea of getting married there—it seems right." Rourk couldn't believe she had changed her mind. He had been prepared to wait years.

"We'll all have time off for Thanksgiving. Is that too soon? I don't know if I'll be able to find a dress that quickly since it's only a little over a month away." Keegan felt a sudden urge to call her mother. She wished Anna and Lauren hadn't left they could go in search of a dress. Her mind was running a mile a minute.

"It's not soon enough as far as I'm concerned."

Keegan laid her head down on his chest and could hear his heart beating loudly. "I love you," she whispered.

Rourk pulled her tight. "Go call your mom. You know you want to."

"You read my mind." She reached in her pocket and pulled out her phone.

Rourk smiled as she paced back and forth, chattering away to her mother. She finally ended the call. "She's over the moon, and she started ticking off a list of things we had to take care of. I didn't realize so much went into planning a wedding. As far as I'm concerned it could just be us and my family. I'd be happy. I don't need anything elaborate."

"I'm sure it will be perfect. I guess I'll have to ask Tommy to be my best man."

"Oh goodness. I wonder if I can have two maids of honor? I can't pick between Anna and

Lauren!" Keegan could feel the panic rising in her chest.

"You'll figure something out. They'll understand no matter what you decide."

"You're right. I'll deal with that later. For now, I want to enjoy spending the day with you before we have to be separated again." She reached for his hand and they headed for the exit together.

"I wonder how Athena is doing? I hate that I had to leave her for so long."

"I'm sure she is doing fine. It was just a few days. You can always call and check up on her if you're worried."

"That's a great idea."

Keegan scrolled to find the kennel's number and dialed. She talked on the phone for a couple of minutes before thanking the person on the other end and hanging up. "She's fine. All the kennel workers love her. The little runt probably doesn't even miss us."

Rourk laughed.

"Let's walk instead of taking the car. I saw they had a bike rental shop; we can really be tourists," Keegan said.

"That sounds like fun."

Keegan wrapped her arm around Rourk's waist as they walked, their feet in perfect rhythm. She shivered at the chill in the air, but it was nothing compared to Alaska. The cool air felt refreshing. She randomly pulled Rourk into some of the little stores and picked up some knick-knacks. Keegan found a beautiful green amber necklace for her mother. She pulled out her phone and looked up the meaning on Google. She smiled when she saw it was rare and often a favorite for healers to help with chronic ailments.

Pushing the door open to the bike shop, they were met with a loud bell as they entered. Keegan laughed when she saw the bikes were all bright orange, old-school cruisers. She asked for one with a basket in case they found more shops. She wouldn't let Rourk take off without getting a photo of him on the bike. He looked so out of place riding it.

He led the way to a bike trail that meandered along the coast. The view was stunning—rugged cliffs that lined the coast so that the ocean crashed against them. Keegan skidded the bike to a stop over and over to take photos. She couldn't wait to add them to her travel collection. There was just something about seaside towns that she found so relaxing, and being with Rourk made it perfect. They spent hours riding around and enjoying each other's company. As usual, the day went too quickly.

Saying goodbye was not getting any easier.

Keegan's heart felt like it was tearing in shreds when they separated at the airport. She glanced at her watch—she still had an hour and twenty minutes before her plane would leave. Of course, she and Rourk were on different concourses. She was hungry, so she slowly trudged to a little shop to grab a snack. She noticed a wedding magazine on the rack and flipped through it. Unable to resist, she added it to her purchases. She still couldn't believe she was going to get married in a little over a month. What she *really* couldn't believe was the idea didn't freak her out at all. She was young, but so what? So were all the other elves that got married. They seemed to be doing fine. She couldn't imagine her life without Rourk in it.

Keegan picked up her phone and called Anna to fill her in on the news.

"Guess what?"

"No idea. You saw the yeti?"

"Close. Rourk and I are going to get married next month!"

"Seriously? That's awesome, Keegan. I'm envious of you guys. I guess that means we won't be roommates."

Keegan hadn't even thought of that. "I'm sorry. I didn't even think of that. I was really looking forward living with you."

"It's ok. You're a slob anyway and that would have driven me crazy."

"I've gotten better." Keegan laughed.

"I'll just find a studio for myself. I have to get out of these dorms. At least we'll be in the same city. So, what's the big plan?"

Keegan told her how she wanted to get married on Thanksgiving break at her parents' property.

"The timing is great since we all planned on going home for the holidays. Don't make me wear a horrendous bridesmaid dress. I'm serious, no bright yellow or big ruffles."

Keegan paced around the seating area. There was so much planning she hadn't thought about. "I promise your dress won't be ugly."

"Make sure Rourk brings some of his hot military friends."

"You're too much, Anna. Ok—I'm at the airport. I'll call you soon. I can't wait to see you again."

Keegan still had time to kill, so she opened her magazine. Most of the dresses were way too fancy for her taste. She pictured herself wearing a flowing, simple ivory gown in chiffon. She could feel the stress rising when she wondered if she would have time to find the perfect dress. Her body temperature was quickly dropping. Taking a few deep breaths, she tried to center herself; she closed her eyes and thought of Rourk. Her body relaxed when she pictured him walking onto the plane. He stopped mid-step and smiled. She knew he realized she was thinking about him. Crisis averted—she didn't freeze the airport. That would not be good, especially with all the cameras and security. *Imagine explaining* that *to Mom.*

Chapter 17

Keegan wasn't sure how she made it through the week without Rourk. It felt like the longest week of her life. Her classes dragged on. The only thing that made time speed up was when she volunteered at the wildlife shelter. Having the computers certainly helped, but it just wasn't the same.

This weekend, they were meeting in Washington, and Rourk was bringing his friend Tommy so they could check out the area and the apartments Tommy had seen online. Keegan was excited to meet a friend of Rourk's. She still couldn't get over his close call with the accident and was very grateful that her mother was a healer. She was also a little nervous—she felt like she needed Tommy's approval.

Anna was waiting outside the gate when Keegan came out of the security checkpoint. Anna had once again morphed her looks. Today, she had an ultra short pixie cut and her hair was almost black. Her crazy green eyes stood out even more with her dark hair and light skin.

Keegan squeezed her tightly. "Your hair looks amazing. I have no idea how you can pull off so many looks. You're like a chameleon."

"Please tell me this isn't your attempt to hook me up on a blind date with Rourk's buddy."

"You wish!" Keegan laughed. The thought had crossed her mind, but she wanted to meet Tommy before she pawned him off on one of her best friends. She wanted to make sure he was good enough for her.

"You're right, I was hoping." Anna bumped Keegan with her hip. They laughed and headed to a nearby cafe.

They caught up and talked about the wedding plans. "I think we'll just let Lauren pick out the dress, if that's ok with you?" Keegan raised an eyebrow.

"Let me think about this. I could spend hours trying on dresses or let Lauren pick. I think I'll go with Lauren."

Keegan nodded. "As much as I hate to admit it, she does have the best taste out of the three of us."

"You won't hear me complaining." Anna bit into a peanut butter cookie, and then filled Keegan in on the apartment she had just rented. Keegan couldn't recall the last time Anna had been so exited about something. She was curious to see if the place lived up to Anna's descriptions. One of her new witch friends had recommended it, and Keegan was certain magic had been involved in securing the apartment and moving in so fast.

Keegan was getting anxious to see Rourk. As

much as she enjoyed seeing one of her best friends, time seemed to stop when she was waiting for her chosen. She kept glancing around and checking the clock on her phone. When she wasn't with Rourk, it was as if the clocks stopped, and sadly, time sped up when he was around.

"He'll be here soon. Calm down," Anna chastised, reaching across the table and snagging Keegan's phone.

Keegan touched the necklace she had grown to love. "I know. I just miss him so much."

Rourk was impatient to see Keegan. Tommy was talking his ear off, but he only heard half of what he was saying. He tried to nod at the appropriate times. He realized he was tapping his foot and immediately planted his foot firmly on the ground. Keegan was the only person that had been able to get under his skin. He didn't feel in control when it came to her. Not that he minded. When was this plane going to land? He looked at his watch yet again.

Finally, he heard the landing gears and a wave of relief washed over him. It wouldn't be long now. The excitement was building in his chest as they walked towards the greeting area.

Keegan raced to him as soon as he passed security. He loved that she was as excited as he was to be back with her. "I missed you," he whispered in her ear.

"It felt like it took you forever to get here." She pressed her body to his.

"I know." He buried his head in her hair inhaling her scent.

Tommy cleared his throat. "Are you going to

introduce me or what?"

Rourk jerked away from Keegan and cleared his throat. "I'm sorry. I forgot you were here."

"Thanks..."

"Keegan, this is Tommy—my friend I've told you about."

Keegan took in the tall, slender blond boy with kind blue eyes and freckles scattered across his face. There was nothing remarkable about him, but he had an infectious smile. She found herself liking him immediately. Keegan turned to introduce Anna, but she wasn't there.

Where did she go? Keegan glanced around and didn't see her anywhere. Great. She grabbed her phone out of her pocket to find out where she went and noticed she had a text from her.

Went to get the car meet you out front.

"Anna's waiting out front." Keegan wrapped her arm around Rourk's waist and smiled up at him. "Let's go. Where is your hotel?"

"We got a place close to Anna's to try to limit the inconvenience."

"That was a great idea."

Keegan steered them towards Anna's old beat-up brown Buick. She had no idea how that thing was still running, or how it had made the cross-country trip. Anna jumped out and ran around to open the trunk. She looked up and nearly bumped into Tommy. "Oh."

Tommy inhaled sharply. "You're Anna?"

She nodded slowly. "You're Tommy?"

They reached for the trunk at the same time and pulled back their hands quickly as they touched.

"You shocked me!" Anna laughed.

"You shocked me. You're, like, electric." Tommy gave her a crooked grin.

Rourk and Keegan watched the exchange. There was obviously a mutual attraction going on. *Maybe I'm not so bad at match making after all*, Keegan thought with a smirk.

As if Rourk knew what she was thinking, he grinned and shook his head while he opened the front door for her. "Stay out of it." He reached down and kissed her, and she wished they were alone. It was going to be hard to share him this weekend. She wanted him all to herself.

Anna took off down the road. She kept glancing in the mirror at Tommy and smiling. Keegan couldn't believe it—she had never seen Anna take to someone so quickly. It was good to see that she had moved on from her long time obsession with Xavier.

Keegan turned in her seat. "Do you guys want to be dropped off at the hotel or go to Anna's for a bit?"

"I'm not in a rush to get to the hotel. I'd like to see where Anna lives." Tommy looked at Rourk. "If that's ok with you."

"Apartment sounds good." Rourk had just got Keegan; he wasn't ready to part ways.

Keegan turned back and gave him a grateful smile.

Tommy leaned forward in his seat and draped his arm over the front seat. "So, do you like living in Washington?"

Anna glanced over her shoulder and flashed him a dazzling smile. "I love it here. It's so beautiful, even with all the rain. There's so much to do outdoors and tons of cool coffee shops."

"Eyes on the road before you get us killed," Keegan said, poking Anna in the arm.

Anna gripped the steering wheel tightly, her eyes back on the road. "You're right. I just get so excited about this place. It's home now."

"How far is your apartment from here?" Tommy asked.

"It's not too far. About another twenty-five minutes." Anna turned up the radio and tapped her fingers along with the music. She kept glancing at the guy in the backseat. She had joked about meeting Rourk's friend, but she had no idea he would be so incredible sexy. He probably thought she was a weirdo. She never had any luck with guys.

Anna eased the car into her parking lot. She couldn't remember if she had picked up around her place before she left or not. She had been too excited to see Keegan. Oh, well. Too late to do anything about it now.

The guys grabbed their backpacks and followed Anna and Keegan up the cobblestone walkway. Keegan was surprised by the flowers that paved the way. There were daisies and peonies in a variety of colors, flanked by bushy spider plants and tall, yellow black-eyed Susans. The lawn was emerald green.

"Anna, how do you keep your flowers alive?" Keegan asked. "I can't even keep a houseplant for more than a couple of weeks."

"Magic," Anna replied casually.

Keegan sucked in a breath and looked at Tommy to see his reaction. He was unfazed. It must have gone over his head—or he thought she was joking.

"Good one." Keegan laughed.

Anna fumbled with her keys and unlocked the small, bright blue door. She pushed it open, switching on the light as they walked though.

Keegan gasped—it was beautiful. Anna's new home was a tiny studio apartment that felt like a hidden oasis. Pots of herbs perched on all the windowsills and crystals were scattered around every available surface. A small altar occupied a corner of the living area; Celtic music played softly in the background. The whole apartment smelled of patchouli. She still had a few unpacked boxes in the corner.

The place seemed like it was made especially for Anna. It was obvious that she loved the place from the way she cared for it—from the pressed pagan tapestries on the walls to the shiny, clean hardwood floors. Keegan could see why Anna had fallen in love with it.

"Do you guys want coffee?" Anna threw her keys on the counter and walked into the kitchen.

"Sure. I could use a cup." Tommy dropped his bag at the doorway and followed her to the kitchen.

Keegan and Rourk looked at each other and shared a smile. Keegan pulled him towards the black suede futon. "I'm so glad you're here."

"Me too." He buried his head in her hair. "I missed your smell."

Keegan laughed. His voice sent chills down her spine.

"Just think—next month, I will be Mrs. Kavanagh. Keegan Kavanagh. I like the sound of it."

"We'll have to start calling you K-squared."

Tommy laughed as he walked back into the room.

"K-squared has a nice ring to it." Anna trailed behind him, holding a mug in her hand. "Do you guys want a cup? If so, help yourselves."

Rourk glanced at Keegan. "Want me to make you one?"

"Sure. Milk and two sugars. And no one is calling me K-squared."

Rourk stood up, and Tommy went with him, staying silent until they were in the kitchen. "Holy shit, Rourk. Why didn't you tell me that Anna was a goddess? I don't think I've ever met anyone so incredible in my life."

"I never noticed." Rourk shrugged. He opened several cabinets searching for Anna's coffee mugs before Tommy indicated the right one.

"Never noticed? It's blinding," Tommy said in a hushed tone.

"I feel the same way about Keegan. She's the only thing I notice when she is around." Rourk looked over the counter at Keegan who was sitting on the couch with her feet tucked beneath her while she talked to an animated Anna.

"I'm sure she's way out of my league." Tommy's face fell as his eyes drifted to Anna.

Rourk stirred Keegan's coffee and poured himself a cup—he drank it black. In the military, you didn't always have the luxury of milk and sugar.

"You never know until you try. Stranger things have happened," Rourk finally answered, thinking of Tommy's miraculous recovery. He narrowed his eyes as he tapped the spoon on Keegan's mug. "She's Keegan's best friend. Don't even think of hurting her."

"Duly noted. I doubt she'd even give me the time of day."

Rourk put the spoon in the sink and went back to the sitting area. It wasn't exactly new territory, the fact that Tommy was always going on about girls. Rourk just wanted to be with Keegan. Tommy could take care of himself.

He handed the cup to Keegan and their hands brushed; she smiled when the tingling sensation shot through her from the contact. Her smile was luminous.

The four of them sat and talked for an hour, catching up. Keegan found it amusing to watch the attraction between Anna and Tommy. She caught them stealing glances at each other several times. Who would have guessed it?

Chapter 18

When his third mug was empty, Rourk patted Keegan's leg and smiled. "Are you ready to check out some apartments? If we don't get started soon, we'll have to push it off till tomorrow."

"I thought you would never ask."

Anna sighed. "I guess that means I have to get up. It's so nice having company."

Tommy pulled a notebook from his backpack. "Do you know where this apartment is?"

She took the paper and stared at it. "Not really. But we can plug it into the GPS and it will show us the way."

Tommy laughed. "Well, I have a few different ones I'd like to check out, if you don't mind?"

"I'm at your service. You ask, and you shall receive."

"Anna, watch what you say around this one," Rourk warned with a grin.

"He's right. A beautiful girl like you..." Tommy winked. "Shouldn't say things like that. I might take it literally."

Anna's face flushed red. "Let's go before I say something I might regret."

As everyone gathered their belongings, Anna grabbed her car keys from the table by the door. They were lying next to a huge amethyst geode.

"Nice rock," Tommy said as he hefted his bag on his shoulder.

Anna narrowed her eyes. "It's not just a rock. It's a crystal."

"Sorry." He held his hands up in mock surrender. "It's pretty, that's all I'm saying."

Anna rolled her eyes and pushed him towards the door.

Tommy had made several appointments before Keegan had decided it was time to get married. So, even though he and Rourk weren't looking to live together anymore, they figured browsing together would accomplish just as much as if they did it separately.

The first place they checked out did not live up to the brochures. The smell of fried foods and cigarettes hit them as they walked through the main entrance. An older lady with graying hair sat behind the counter. Her eyes were wide-set and her nose was crooked—like it had been broken but never reset. Tommy told her he had made an appointment online to check out an apartment. She reached under the counter and pulled out a key.

Rourk thought there was no way in hell he was going to live in this dump with Keegan. The elevator shook as they headed to the sixth floor.

"It looked so nice on the website," Tommy mumbled under his breath.

"We're here. We might as well check it out. Maybe it will surprise us," Keegan said.

Tommy fiddled with the key a couple minutes and finally pushed the door open. They walked into the empty foyer. There was wallpaper peeling off the wall and brown spots on the ceiling. The carpet was so old and dirty that the color was indistinguishable.

"Who uses wallpaper anymore?" Keegan asked as she ran her hand down the wall. It felt sticky.

The rest of the apartment was more of the same. They just did a quick walk through and crossed it off the list. The woman didn't seem too surprised when they handed the key back and said they were going to check out some other places first.

The next place they went to was much better. The price was quite a bit higher, and the apartments were pretty small, but at least they were clean. They peeked into the gym first, and then went in the back to see the pool before they looked upstairs.

Tommy glanced around the living room. "I like it. It's much bigger than our barracks, and the gym is top notch. Really all I need is a clean place and somewhere to workout. There are lots of hiking trails, too. Plus, it's not too big for just me."

Rourk walked into the kitchen and turned on the faucet. The water ran clear, and it heated up quickly.

Anna looked at Keegan. "What do you think?"

"It's ok. I'd still like to see the other two places."

Rourk nodded his head in agreement.

The next place they didn't even bother to go in. There were bars on all the windows. Never a good sign. Anna turned the car around without a word, and they plugged on to the next location.

As soon as they pulled up, Keegan knew it would be her home with Rourk. A private gate opened to a landscape that was breathtaking: lush plants and colorful flowers placed strategically around meandering paths. But, that wasn't what caught Keegan's eye: it was the waterfall she could hear in the distance. It made her feel like she was home. "This is it Rourk."

He laughed. "We haven't even been inside."

"I don't care. I can feel it. This is where we are meant to be."

He draped his arm around her shoulder. "We'll at least look at it before we sign the papers. Ok?"

"I guess I can agree to that." She grinned up at him and threw her arm around his waist. "This will be our first home as a married couple."

Rourk leaned down and kissed the top of her head. "We need to make sure they accept pets."

"Oh, they better!" Keegan marched up to the counter. She narrowed her eyes at the young man behind it. "Do you allow pets?"

He pushed his glasses back further on his nose. "Yes. But you have to put down a pet deposit. Which is one month's rent."

"That's pretty steep." Keegan said.

He shrugged his shoulder and looked back down at his paperwork.

"We'd like to check out a two-bedroom."

"Do you want to see a villa or an apartment?"

Keegan looked up at Rourk questioningly.

"Whatever you want."

"We'd like to see a villa." The man made a phone call, and a tall blond woman wearing too much make-up came out to meet them. She towered over Keegan. "My name is Lisa, and I'll be your tour guide today." It was obviously a well-rehearsed line, and it looked awkward on her face. She had probably gone overboard on the Botox. "Right this way. You're in luck—we do have a villa open. They usually go quickly."

Keegan rolled her eyes. They probably said that to everyone.

They walked through the apartment building and out the back door. Keegan sucked in her breath. A sense of calmness came over her as she stepped foot on the stone pathway. Off in the distance, she could see little wooden bungalows. That was the only way she could think to describe them. They had small porches, each with two wooden chairs and a matching table that appeared to be made of branches. She squeezed Rourk's hand, and he squeezed back. There was enough distance between each bungalow to give a sense of privacy.

"1303 is open. It's at the back of the property, so I'm afraid you will have a walk in the morning to get to your vehicles. Would that be a problem?"

"Not at all," Rourk replied.

Keegan looked back at Anna with a big grin. Anna gave her the thumbs-up.

The woman wasn't kidding that it was a walk. About ten minutes later, they reached 1303 tucked in the back of the complex. Keegan felt the excitement rise in her chest. The closer they got to the bungalow, the louder the rushing water from the waterfall. She didn't dare ask the woman about it. Besides, it would be much more exciting for Rourk and her to find it on their own.

Once they reached the doorway, the woman turned the key and pushed the door open. Keegan could have squealed with delight. It was small, but cozy. The first thing she noticed was the skylight. The walls were light mocha, and the kitchen was modern with matching stainless-steel appliances. The woman led them into the master bedroom—it was bigger than her room in Alaska. What really took Keegan by surprise was the bathroom. Smooth stones covered the walls, and it had a deep sunken tub. She ran her hand over the antique-looking faucet.

It really was perfect. Keegan smiled. "We'll take it."

Rourk laughed. The realtor turned and looked at him.

"What's the monthly rate?" he asked.

Lisa told him a figure and he grimaced. It was over his monthly housing allowance. He looked over at Keegan; her face was flushed with excitement. He had been saving a lot of money since he joined the military. "Where do we sign? We won't be moving here until December, will that be a problem?"

"Only if you mind paying for it until you move in. I can't hold it. If you want to take the villa, your rent starts on the day you sign on the dotted line."

"So we could stay the night here if we wanted?" Keegan's eyes widened.

"As long as you fill out the paperwork and

pay the deposits, you will get the keys today."

Keegan clapped her hands together. She turned and looked up at Rourk, her blue-green eyes dancing with excitement. "Can we?"

Rourk knew he wouldn't be able to say no. He just nodded. "Of course. Let's get it today."

"I'm sure it's going to take a while for you guys to do the paperwork," Tommy cut in. "Is it ok if Anna takes me back to the other apartment so I can see about securing one for December? If that's ok with Anna."

Anna smiled at him. "I'd love to. We can grab something to eat too."

After they arrived back at the complex's main building, they said their goodbyes and parted ways. Rourk and Keegan were led down a hallway to Lisa's office to sign papers. Keegan was beyond thrilled. Soon, they would be married and living together. Her childhood dream was coming true. She glanced over at Rourk—he was so much more than any fantasy she had made up as a little girl. She stared at his rugged profile and had to consciously stop herself from running her fingers down his strong jaw line.

He caught her eyes on him, and his lips curved into the slightest smile. He knew she was thinking about him. After several faxes back and forth between the bank—and many signatures later—Lisa handed them the keys. "It's all yours. At least until your lease runs out."

"Thank you!" Keegan snatched the dangling keys and looked down at them in her hand. They really did it; the place was theirs. She held the keys up and shook them at Rourk. "We need to go shopping to furnish our home."

Rourk pictured Keegan's brightly colored apartment with its strange, globe lanterns and fluffy rugs. "What do you say we go with a look that matches the villa? Keep it earth tones and natural looking?"

"That's a great idea!" As they walked back out into the sunlight, Keegan rambled on about simplistic looks she had seen in magazines and stores that used only recycled materials.

Rourk tried to hide his relief and smile. He wasn't sure he could handle a living room with fuzzy pink pillows.

"Let's go home." Keegan grabbed Rourk's hand and tugged him towards the path that led to their new home. "We have to find that waterfall."

"I knew you were thinking that." Rourk looked up at the sky. "The sun is setting. Why don't we save it for tomorrow? I don't think it's very far from our place."

"Do you want to stay here tonight?" Keegan asked.

Rourk hesitated. "We don't have anywhere to sleep. Maybe we should wait till tomorrow or the next visit."

"We could go shopping tonight and buy a mattress and sheets."

Rourk grabbed both of her hands; they always felt so warm. He didn't know if it was just her body heat or the connection between them. "Keegan, I know you are used to having everything you want. Believe me, I want to be able to give you anything you desire. But, I don't think you've seen a soldier's pay check. You are going to have to get used to having less. The rent alone is going to eat up a huge chunk."

Keegan was surprised. "Rourk, money is something we will never have to worry about. My uncle has set up funds for all the children. You know he is wise with numbers."

Rourk pulled his hands back. "Keegan, I don't want us to live off your family's money. I want to support you on my own."

"It's not their money. It's mine. As soon as I turned eighteen, I got access to my trust fund. Having this money allows us to travel. For you to be a solider and not have to worry about how we are going to pay the electric bill. My father has no problem with it. My uncle uses his mental gift to help his family. There is no shame in that."

Rourk considered Keegan's words. It still didn't set right with him. However, he knew as a soldier he would never be able to provide Keegan with the lifestyle she was used to. "You can use your money to buy extras and travels, but I insist on paying the bills and providing food for the table."

Keegan chuckled. "You're so old-fashioned. I love it. And it's our money."

They spent the next hour or so talking about where they would put the furniture. Rourk paced off the measurements, and Keegan entered them into her notes on her phone. She kept track of how many curtains they would need and tried to compile a list for kitchen and bathroom supplies—although she was sure she was forgetting things. There were big purchases to be made, too, like a washer and dryer. So many things to do.

Keegan's phone went off in her hand—Anna was on her way to pick them up. She hated to leave, but agreed that it made more sense to start shopping tomorrow in the daylight. It wouldn't be easy getting the furniture down the stone pathway in the dark, after all.

Chapter 19

Keegan ended up staying the night at Anna's. She would have rather stayed with Rourk, but he got a hotel room with Tommy.

"So what do you think of Tommy?" Keegan grinned and crossed her legs on the couch. The television was playing softly in the background. She sipped her mug of hot cocoa; she hadn't felt so relaxed in a long time.

"Keegan, I don't know what to think. I've never been so attracted to anyone before. Even with Xavier. That obsession grew out of knowing him since I was young. This was instant, and it took me by surprise. He's hot, isn't he?"

Keegan pictured Tommy in her mind, and hot was not one of the words that came to mind. Maybe because he was Rourk's best friend, she couldn't think of him that way. "He seems nice, and Rourk thinks he's great. That says a lot about him."

"I wonder what he thinks of me?" Anna

reached for a handful of popcorn.

"That's a ridiculous question. The attraction was obviously mutual."

"Seriously? Are you just saying that? I didn't get that vibe from him."

"Then you're blind." Keegan flipped through the channels. After a few moments of staring blankly at a sitcom, she glanced over at Anna. "This is nice. I miss our girl time."

"Me too. Childhood friends are impossible to replace. Even the witches I meet here, they're cool, but it's just not the same. I miss Lauren, too."

Rourk and Tommy showed up bright and early. Keegan jumped out of bed as soon as the knock sounded—seeing Rourk was well worth getting up early. She threw her hair in a ponytail and hurried out to join her friends.

He met her with a big smile and a kiss. The smell of coffee filled the room. Anna had a huge spread of fruit on the table and was standing at the counter cracking eggs. It was hard to believe they were all growing up and living on their own.

"Do you need any help?" Rourk asked.

"Don't tell me you cook too? Keegan, why haven't you married this man yet?"

"Soon. Speaking of, Anna and I are going to have to go off on our own today in search of *the dress.*"

Anna turned to Tommy and mouthed. *Help me!*

"I saw that." Keegan stuck her tongue out at Anna. "It won't be that bad. We'll set a cap of two hours. I don't want to be apart from Rourk any longer than needed."

"I guess I can live with two hours." Anna carried the plate of scrambled eggs to the table.

"Rourk, we gotta hit those trails while we have the chance," Tommy begged.

"You read my mind." Rourk reached over and scooped some fruit onto his plate.

"Hiking doesn't get much better. I feel at one with nature when I'm outside." Anna said wistfully. "Take a poncho. You can pretty much count on it raining as soon as you step foot in the woods."

Keegan was frustrated when she climbed into Anna's car. "Two hours and nothing!"

"I think you're being too picky. There were some very pretty dresses. You looked beautiful in them all."

Keegan sighed and threw her head back on the seat. "They were ok, but they weren't *the dress*. You know when you're little you always dream of finding the perfect dress. When you slip it on, you just know it's the one."

"Not all little girls dream of their wedding day. I'll probably get married in jeans."

"You wouldn't dare!" Keegan laughed, but cut it short as she reconsidered. "Never mind, I wouldn't be surprised."

"What are you and Rourk going to do for the rest of the day?"

"I know we're going to search for that waterfall at the apartment complex, and maybe do some furniture shopping. Do you mind keeping Tommy busy? I feel bad since you just met him."

"That's fine. I'll show him around, and we'll grab something to eat." She grinned over at

Keegan. "I'd like to get to know more about him anyway."

Keegan texted Rourk and let him know they were on the way. He replied that they were going to meet them at Anna's.

When they pulled in, Rourk and Tommy were waiting at the door. Keegan's face lit up at the sight of him, and her heart rate accelerated.

"Any luck?" Rourk asked.

"Nope. Maybe next time." Keegan tried to keep the frustration out of her voice, but didn't think she succeeded.

"You'll find something." Rourk reached for her hand. "What do you want to do first?"

Keegan looked up at the sky it was a beautiful crisp morning and not a rain cloud in sight. "We should probably go in search of the waterfall first."

"I was hoping you would say that." Rourk turned towards Anna. "Do you mind dropping us off at the apartment? We could call a cab."

"Don't be ridiculous. Of course I don't mind. I wanted to show Tommy around that area anyway."

Rourk held open the back door for her. She slid in and scooted to the middle to be closer to him.

"I wonder how far away it is?" Keegan asked as she listened to the soothing sound of the falls.

"I don't think it's too far away." Rourk led her into the woods. He walked soundlessly, but Keegan's footsteps were loud and cumbersome.

Keegan glanced around and took in the beautiful wilderness that surrounded her. She loved the feeling of peace that washed over her when she was closest to nature. She heard animals scurry as they approached. The sun shone brightly through the forest. Keegan tilted her face up and felt the warmth on her skin. Even though the air was chilly, she pictured the warmth of the sun and it radiated throughout her body. She loved being an elf.

They were well off the beaten path. She trusted Rourk's instincts. The sound of rushing water grew near and excitement filled her chest. She squeezed Rourk's hand, smiling at him.

"I love how excited you get. You're like a little kid; it's cute."

Keegan giggled and looked around wistfully. "I can't explain it..."

"You don't have to—I feel the same way. I'm just better at masking my emotions than you are."

Keegan's thoughts drifted to their handfasting. "Are you nervous about getting married?"

Rourk stopped in his tracks and turned towards her. "Why would I be nervous?"

"I don't know, I thought it was common to get cold feet. At least that's what they always show on the movies. The guy freaking out about being tied down to the same person for the rest of his life."

Rourk chuckled. "Not one fiber of my being is nervous about marrying you. In my eyes, we are already married. This is a formality to tell the world and to honor our ancestors with the tradition. I've never wanted anything more than to be united with you, Keegan. You are my chosen, the only woman I will ever love."

Keegan stared up at his rugged face and into

his intense grey eyes and knew he spoke the truth. She reached up and lightly traced his lips. Rourk pulled her close, pressing his body firmly to hers as their lips met. Keegan's body felt weak with desire. She couldn't wait until she could experience him fully.

Rourk pulled away and smiled down at her. "Soon," he whispered as he lightly brushed her hair off her shoulder.

She wondered if he had read her thoughts or if it was just that obvious. She felt the heat rising in her cheeks. She smiled recklessly and took off in a run, dodging the fallen trees and feeling the wind through her hair. She felt alive. Rourk laughed, a sharp burst of sound in the stillness of the forest, and gave chase behind her. She wasn't sure where she was going, but she ran till her legs ached. It was as if something was guiding her and she was along for the ride.

Her breathing labored, she finally came to an abrupt stop. "It's here." She pointed into a thick patch of trees and shrubs that were not meant to be walked through.

Rourk walked ahead of her and pushed through the thick undergrowth, holding branches back for her as he advanced. The sounds of the falls grew stronger. Finally, they broke through to a clearing. Keegan gasped—they were standing on the edge of a ledge, and below them was a wild, rushing water fall at least 50 feet tall. Mother Nature never ceased to amaze her. She was at a loss for words as she and Rourk stood, hands clasped, taking in the beauty.

"Can we get closer?" Keegan asked eagerly.

"We could, but I think we'll leave that for

another day. We don't have the proper gear. Now we know where it is, so we can come back often."

"Our spot." Her eyes shone with excitement.

"Yes. Our spot," Rourk repeated as he draped his arm around her shoulder and pulled her closer.

They stood for a long time in silence, staring at the magnificent waterfall as the sun began to sink.

Rourk looked up as a drop of rain hit his cheek. "The rain comes so unexpectedly here. We need to head back."

Keegan closed her eyes and inhaled deeply, wanting to take the peace and tranquility back with her. Opening her eyes, she looked up at her chosen and nodded. Rourk quickened his step as the rain started to pelt down on them. He was upset with himself for not bringing rain gear. He worried about Keegan getting sick. Rourk glanced back at her and grinned. Even with her hair plastered to her head, she was still the most beautiful creature he had ever laid eyes on. He gave her hand a soft squeeze and continued forward. When he looked at her he didn't see the young girl that she was now, he saw the woman she would become: strong, loving, loyal, and full of adventure. He didn't know what he did to deserve to spend the rest of his life with her, but he was thankful.

It took them about an hour to make their way back to their villa. Rourk fumbled with the key, anxious to get Keegan inside so she could warm up. He pushed the door open and let her go first. "I'm sorry I wasn't prepared for the rain. I should have known better." Rourk shook his head in disgust.

"It was fun." Keegan peeled off her jacket and rubbed her hands together to generate warmth. "Thanks for catching me. If it weren't for you, I would have fallen at least twice."

"I doubt that. You underestimate yourself at times, Keegan. The way you found the falls was impressive. I think it would have taken me longer."

"You're just saying that." She kicked off her shoes. "It was pretty strange. As if the falls were calling to me."

"They probably were." Rourk glanced around the living room. He smiled ruefully. "This is not good. We have no dry clothes or towels. Maybe we should have gone shopping first."

"At least there's heat. I'm going to take a hot shower. I'm chilled to my bones."

"Throw your clothes out here, and I'll put them in front of the fire place."

Keegan got undressed and tossed her clothes outside the door. They didn't even have a shower curtain so she turned on the bath instead. She ran the water as hot as she could stand it and sunk into the tub, letting her head relax on the rim. *It should be illegal to be this content*, she thought, as the warmth radiated throughout her body. She eased herself lower in the tub until her head was completely submerged. *That feels much better.* Her scalp was no longer tingling from the cold. After soaking for about twenty minuets, the water was starting to cool so she pulled herself out of the sunken tub.

She looked around and realized it was not a well thought-out plan. She was dripping wet and not a towel in sight. She tiptoed to the door and cracked it open. "Rourk, we have no towels."

She watched as he ran his hand through his hair and looked around trying to figure out what to do. He pulled off his undershirt and handed it to her through the crack. "That's the best I have until our clothes dry or Anna gets here. Sorry."

"That's fine." Keegan grabbed the white shirt from his hands and closed the door quickly before she pulled him inside.

Keegan put the T-shirt to her face and inhaled his scent. She grinned to herself and thought, *It smells like rain.*

She used the shirt to blot the water off her body and stood there in the bathroom, starting to shiver. *Now what?*

She pulled his shirt over her head. It was wet, but it was the only option and at least it wasn't freezing like her other clothes. Slowly, she opened in the door and walked out to the living room.

Rourk looked up and inhaled deeply, unable to look away. For a long moment, his gaze held hers. He stayed rooted in his spot, and she advanced. By the look in his eyes, Keegan knew he was teetering on losing self-control. She was so tempted to take advantage of the situation. But she knew how important waiting till they said their vows was to him, so she broke the silence. "You go ahead and jump in the shower, and I'll call Anna." She busied herself moving the clothes around in front of the fire.

She heard his footsteps and then the door shutting. This was not a good predicament to be in. There had to be something she could do. Suddenly, she had an idea. She pulled on her wet jeans and jacket and ran over to the nearest neighbors.

The door was answered right away. An older woman with grey hair and sad brown eyes opened the door.

"I'm sorry to bother you. We just moved in next door and we got caught in the storm. We haven't bought any goods for the house yet so we don't even have towels. Is it possible I could borrow a towel?"

The woman checked Keegan over, as if to make sure she was a trustworthy person, then smiled. "Come in. Of course you can borrow a towel. I'll be right back." The woman hurried to the back of the villa and came out holding two fluffy pink towels.

Keegan reached for them and gave her a grateful smile. "Thank you so much. I promise I'll return them."

The woman waved her hand. "Don't worry about it dear. I have a closet full of towels and it's just me. You can keep them."

"Oh, well, again—thank you. We're only just now setting up the house, but once we move in next month, maybe you can come over for lunch?" Keegan said.

The woman smiled warmly, and it reached her eyes making her look beautiful. "That would be wonderful."

"I hate to take your towels and run..."

"Nonsense. You hurry along before you catch a cold."

"Thanks." Keegan waved and ran back to their place.

The water was still running when she walked

in so she tapped lightly on the door. "I got you a towel. I'm going to throw it in ok?"

He must not have heard her because there was no reply. She opened the door just a crack and threw the towel in.

Standing in front of the fire place, Keegan shimmied out of her jeans and set them back down to dry off. She wrapped the towel around her and waited for Rourk to come out.

She laughed when he entered the room in the pink towel wrapped at his waist. She tried not to stare too long at his broad shoulders—she was fearful of caving in herself.

"Where did you get the towels?"

"Neighbor. She seems nice. I also called Anna. They should be here in a few moments. They were at her apartment so I told them to bring our backpacks."

Rourk breathed out a sigh of relief. Seeing Keegan almost naked nearly made him come undone. He appreciated the fact that she had defused a situation that could have easily gone a different way. "Thank you."

"I don't want you to have any regrets about our first time together."

"I'm glad you understand."

"I might not agree, but I understand."

"We really need to do some shopping."

"Yes, a kettle is first on our list. I would kill for a cup of tea or cocoa right now."

Rourk smiled gratefully at her. The change of subjects was most welcome.

"I wonder how long before Anna gets here?"

As if on queue, there was a knock at the door. Keegan ran to open it. Anna looked back and forth between them standing in their towels. "Are we interrupting something?"

"Be quiet and get in here." Keegan pulled her by the arm into the house. Tommy was right behind her with the two backpacks slung across his shoulders.

Rourk grabbed Keegan's "You go first."

"Nice towel." Tommy smirked.

Rourk looked at him indifferently as he pulled his dry clothes out of bag.

They spent the rest of the afternoon shopping for their place. When they were done, Anna had them all over for dinner. She made sweet and sour chicken and rice, and it was wonderful. After the boys left to go to their apartment, Anna turned on Keegan. "So? Did you do it?"

Keegan laughed. "Do it? How old are you?"

"I could feel the tension when we walked in. It's been killing me not knowing."

"No, we didn't have sex. I'm going to honor his wishes and wait till we're married."

Anna sighed. "That is pretty romantic."

"What about you and Tommy? Anything?"

Anna's shoulders slumped and she fell into the chair. "Nothing. I was hoping he would try something, but he was a perfect gentlemen. I don't think he's into me."

"Maybe you have to make the first move."

They stayed up, chatting like the old days, and Keegan was sad that they would be leaving the next day. There was so much to do before they moved to Washington.

Chapter 20

Keegan was really starting to stress out.

She had decided to take a few days off classes and go home to Tennessee with Athena in hopes of finding a dress. Rourk was going to meet her there for the weekend. The wedding was only two weeks away, and she hadn't found a gown she loved. She really didn't want to settle with an *ok* dress. It had to be perfect. She was probably driving her mom and the girls crazy, but she couldn't help it.

Her grandmother was sitting at the table with her in her mother's kitchen. "You know, Keegan, in my day we wore blue wedding dresses."

Keegan crinkled up her nose. "Blue?"

"Yes, it was an Irish tradition."

"Really? What did your dress look like?" Keegan was so curious about this. Maybe that's what was wrong in her search for a dress. She was so stuck on finding a white gown that she hadn't bothered to look at anything else. She knew Rourk loved tradition. Maybe she could surprise him with a blue wedding dress.

"Oh, it was beautiful. Long and flowing. I don't think I ever felt more beautiful than on my wedding day," her grandmother said wistfully. "I still have it stored away."

"You do?" Keegan's eyes were wide with surprise. "You have to let me see it."

"We can go see it now if you'd like."

Keegan jumped up and grabbed the keys to her grandmother's car. "What are you waiting for?"

Her grandmother chuckled. "You always were so impatient."

They walked through her grandmother's door and she automatically turned on the hot water for tea. Her mother did the same thing; it made Keegan smile. Keegan followed her down the narrow hall to her bedroom. "It's in the closet."

Keegan waited while her grandmother sorted through the hangers. "Here it is." She pulled out a long white garment bag.

"May I?" Keegan asked.

"Of course, dear. I'm sure it's out dated now. It's been so many years." Her grandmother looked off in the distance, lost in her memories.

Keegan slowly unzipped the bag. She felt like she had found a buried treasure. Energy coursed through her body. She gasped as she lightly took it out of the bag. "Oh, Nanny. It's gorgeous." Keegan held it up to her body and stared at herself in the mirror. "Can I try it on?"

Her grandmother looked her up and down, her eyes scrutinizing her granddaughter. "Sure, I was about your size when I got married. Although I had a little more in the chest department, and you have a little more in the booty department."

Keegan giggled. "Funny. I'll be right back. I can't wait to try this on."

The kettle whistled, and her grandmother hurried away.

Keegan's hands shook when she stepped into the gown. She loved that there was history to the dress. When she couldn't reach to finish zipping the dress, she poked her head from the bedroom and yelled, "Nanny, can you try to zip me up?"

A couple of minutes later, her grandmother walked in to the bathroom. She stopped in her tracks and covered her mouth. "Keegan, you look...magical." She walked behind her and zipped up the dress. "It's a bit lose in the top, but nothing I couldn't fix with thread and a little time."

Keegan looked at her reflection. The dress was a pale blue, the color of robins' eggs. *Ice blue* crossed her mind. The strapless top was flattering to her figure. It was all chiffon, which flowed out on the bottom in soft drapes. A ribbon with a white flower was wrapped twice around her waist.

"Oh Nanny, please let me wear this dress. Nothing else will ever live up to this dress. It's too perfect for words," she begged.

Her grandmother smiled sadly. "I had always hoped one of my daughters would ask to wear it. But you know how they are. They are all so strong-minded they wouldn't think of doing something that wasn't their idea. I would be honored if you would wear this dress at your wedding." She wiped a tear away.

Keegan wrapped her arms around her grandmother and gave her a squeeze. "Thank you. I knew there was a reason I wasn't having any luck finding a dress. There was one waiting for me all along."

Suddenly, the wedding felt real. She had *the dress*. In two weeks, she would be a married woman. She couldn't wait to start her married life with Rourk. When she came back out to the kitchen, her grandmother was gathering knitting supplies.

Keegan reached for the red yarn.

"Of course you would be drawn to the passion cord." Her grandmother chuckled.

"What are you doing?" Keegan pulled out a chair and sat down.

"Making the handfasting cord."

Keegan's eyes widened. "You are making them?"

"Of course who else is going to make it? Your mother? She couldn't knit to save her soul."

"I don't know. I guess I just thought they were bought or made in bulk."

"That's silly! Each one is made specifically for the couple. Once I complete my part, I'll pass it on to your brother, and he will have it charged with magic for good luck."

"What does the blue stand for?"

"Loyalty, honor, and patience. All very important in a marriage."

Elves loved tradition, and handfastings were one of the ways they kept the ancient traditions alive. "What about the broom and sword?"

"We will use a sword of your father's, of course. And the broom will be the one Rourk's parents used at their handfasting."

"Wow." She was deeply touched that they would be using the same broom that Rourk's parents had used. Of course, she also loved the idea of using her father's sword. It would be a beautiful ceremony, and she was genuinely getting anxious for it to arrive.

"What other traditions are there?"

"Oh goodness. Too many to mention. Most of them are small details you wouldn't even notice if not pointed out."

"Such as?" Keegan promoted her to continue.

"Lavender in your bouquet for devotion, the veil to ward off evil spirits, coin in the shoe for wealth, tilt your face to the sun after your vows to have beautiful children, bagpipes, braided hair, bells for gifts... I could go on and on."

Keegan placed her chin in her hands and sighed. "It's going to be a beautiful day, isn't it?"

"Of course. Why don't you get back to your mother's so I can finish up the cords? You can bring the car back tomorrow."

"I can take a hint." Keegan smiled at her grandmother. "Thank you. I can't wait to tell mom about the dress."

"Well, get out of here. I'll see you tomorrow." Her grandmother went back to her knitting, a smile playing across her face.

Keegan rushed into the house. "Mom!"

"Just a minute." Her mother yelled down the stairs. "I have Warrick in the bathtub."

She didn't feel like waiting so she took the stairs two at a time. "I found the dress!"

"Oh Keegan, that's wonderful I was starting

to get concerned. Where is it?" Emerald was perched on the edge of the tub, pouring water over Warrick's head to rinse out the suds.

"It's at Nanny's. She needs to take in the top a little. Well, a lot."

"Where did you find it? I thought we hit all the local stores?"

"You'll never believe it. It's Nanny's wedding dress. It's perfect."

"Oh."

"Oh? That's all you have to say?" Keegan raised an eyebrow.

"I guess I'm just a little sad you didn't ask to try on my dress."

Keegan laughed. "Nanny said the same thing about you and your sisters."

"She did?"

"Yep, it hurt her feelings."

Emerald pulled Warrick out of the tub and toweled him off. He wasn't very happy about it. "I guess I never thought to ask her either. I was so focused on finding a new dress the thought never crossed my mind. I'm glad you asked her. I'm sure it made her happy, and I know you'll look stunning."

Keegan reached for her brother. "I was hoping I could wear your veil. Nanny told me it was to ward off evil sprits. I can't think of two stronger people than you and dad."

Her mother's eyes misted and she leaned forward, wrapping her arms around Keegan and Warrick. "I would be honored if you wore my veil. Let's have some tea and go over the plans. Did you decide what to do about your maid of honor?

"Actually, I did. I'm going to have both of

them since Rourk is having Tommy and Thaddeus. I don't think they need to be labeled. They will be my two best friends standing by my side on one of the most important days of my life."

"That's sweet. Surely they have their dresses by now?"

"Yeah, Lauren picked them out in California. She sent me some pictures they are perfect." Keegan flipped through the photos on her phone, and then handed it to her mother.

"Oh, that is perfect for a fall wedding. Lauren always has the best taste."

Keegan took the phone back and looked down at the silk taffeta, dark brown dress that fell just above the knee. The ruffled crossover collar was what really made the dress. She looked at Lauren for a moment longer; she was positively glowing in the dress. Keegan was curious to meet her boyfriend—Tristen, the dark fairy.

"I have everything taken care of as far as the food, music, and flowers. It's going to be a magical day." Her mother gave a sad smile as she set a cup of tea in front of Keegan. "It's hard to believe my little girl will be tying the knot soon. Seems like just yesterday you were running around in pigtails and getting into mischief."

"I don't think that has changed much—other than the pigtails." Keegan grinned.

"Oh, that's not true. You've grown up a lot. You will continue to blossom." Her mother reached out and put her small, warm hand on top of hers. "Rourk brings out the best in you."

"I definitely feel more centered since the bond has returned."

Thaddeus strolled into the room and sat

down next to Keegan, then nonchalantly asked, "How's Anna?"

"Fine. Why?" Keegan looked at him curiously. She could never tell what her brother was thinking. She knew he worked with Anna to get his bond back so maybe he was just making small talk. But, she always had to wonder if he had seen a vision.

"Just wondering. I know you met up with her last weekend. Didn't Rourk bring Tommy?"

Keegan narrowed her eyes. "Yes, is there something I should know about Tommy? Anna was quite taken with him, and I don't want her to get hurt."

She watched his face intently to see if he would give anything away. His lip twitched as if he wanted to smile, but was fighting the urge.

"Nothing you should know. I haven't had any visions of Tommy causing any trouble for Anna."

Keegan crossed her arms and sat back in the chair. She knew her brother was keeping something from her, but she also knew it was useless to bug him. He never gave away anything he didn't want to.

"I'm just curious how she's doing learning the craft. She's a very powerful witch."

"Oh, well she's found a couple of witches to practice with. She has gotten stronger."

Thaddeus stood up and walked to the counter to grab an apple. "Mom, want me to take Warrick out with me?"

"Where are you going?" Emerald asked.

"Just out in the woods for a walk. I think it's time I start taking him. Quality time."

"That's fine, just be careful. Make sure you

have your phone on you."

Thaddeus rolled his eyes at her and scooped up his brother from floor. "Come on, little guy." He hoisted him on his shoulders causing him to giggle.

"Have fun," Keegan yelled after them.

Keegan and her mother shared a smile.

Athena sat at the door and whimpered when the door shut behind them.

Chapter 21

Rourk showed up on Friday, and Keegan was ecstatic to see him. She longed for the day that they would be together every night. Although, she knew that would never be reality. Even after they were married, he would still have to leave for stretches of time because of his work. Once they were both in Washington, it would get easier. They pulled into her parent's driveway, and Keegan turned towards Rourk.

"Guess what?" She grinned from ear to ear and grabbed him by the arms.

"You found out you have a new power?" Rourk teased.

"Close. I got accepted to the art school in Seattle. I'm changing my major to photography. I'm still going to keep up with my science courses in case I change my mind and want to go back to Biology."

"Keegan, that's great news. I'm proud of you." Rourk leaned over the center console and wrapped his arms around her. "Have you told your parents?"

"Not yet. I keep putting it off. I guess I'll tell them this weekend." Truth be told, she was nervous to tell them. She had no idea how they would react.

"I'm sure they will be happy for you."

"We'll see…"

"Speaking of parents, my father has been giving me a hard time about not seeing us enough. Do you mind coming to his place tonight for dinner?"

"Of course not. I'm sorry I'm so greedy with my time with you. I didn't even think about your dad missing you. We should make something to bring over for desert. What's his favorite?" She loved the idea of cooking something for his father. She was sure he had to be lonely with the house all to himself.

Rourk thought about it for a moment. "I've never seen him turn away homemade chocolate chip cookies."

"Great, that will be easy to make." Keegan pushed open the door and jumped out of her mom's Land Rover. She shivered when the cool air hit her face. She was glad they had a weather manipulator on hand. They would be able to turn up the heat a notch for their outdoor wedding.

"What are you smiling at?" Rourk asked.

"Our wedding. I can't believe we will be married next weekend. It seems too good to be true." Keegan pushed open the front door and let the warmth of the house seep into her body. Athena ran up, wagging her little stub of a tail. Rourk reached down and picked up the puppy.

"Hot chocolate?" Her mother peeked out of the kitchen.

"Definitely. It got cold early this year." Keegan hung her jacket on the rack, and Rourk handed off the dog and did the same. She pulled off her winter cap, and her curls bounced out.

"I didn't notice you cut your hair with it all up in the hat." Rourk reached up and touched a curl. "It looks cute."

"I was inspired by Anna's latest transformation. I'm not quite as daring as her; just went a little shorter."

"You would look great bald."

Keegan laughed. "I wouldn't go that far."

"What are your plans for the day?" Emerald asked.

Keegan glanced over at Rourk. "Not sure. Tonight, we are going over to Rourk's house to have dinner with his father. Speaking of fathers, is dad home? I feel like I haven't seen him in forever."

"He's home. He took the boys out to give me some quiet time."

"Which we are interrupting," Keegan said apologetically.

"Nonsense. I barely get to see you anymore. Sit down, you two, and tell me what's going on in your lives. Rourk, how's work going?" She set a mug of cocoa in front of him, and then took a seat across from Keegan.

"It's a lot of fun. I can see why Richard stayed in so long. The human military is a great community." He picked up the mug to take a sip but when the steam hit his face, he decided to let it cool down. "I'm certainly looking forward to getting to Washington and being placed on a team."

"It's too bad you guys weren't going to be stationed closer." Emerald sighed.

"We'll be back here before you know it. Rourk doesn't plan on staying past his contract. Right?" Keegan raised an eyebrow. Of course, she would go anywhere with him, but she missed her home. A few years away wouldn't be too bad.

"As far as I know, I just serve my term and then come back here to the Army of The Light. Of course, that could change." Rourk lightly squeezed Keegan's leg under the table.

"Speaking of changes. I've decided to change my major to photography." She might as well spit it out while it was just her mother, and Rourk was there to back her up.

"Really?" Her mother took a sip of her cocoa and set the mug down. "You've always wanted to be a marine biologist. Are you sure you want to make that big switch? You haven't really given it a try. I could tell how much you loved working at the sanctuary."

"I've been thinking about it for the last couple of months. Photography makes me happy. I can always go back to school later for biology." Keegan's shoulders slumped in anticipation of her mother's criticism over her choice.

"Well, I think it's a wonderful idea. You are clearly talented, and life is too short to be unhappy."

"Really?" Keegan's mouth hung open. "I thought you would tell me it was a ridiculous idea and be upset that I wasted money on school."

Emerald laughed. "Not at all. It's your life,

you have the right to change your mind if you want to. When I was growing up I wanted to be so many different things. The only reason why I was surprised is because you never wavered on your path until now. Ever since you were old enough to talk, you told me how you wanted to work with dolphins."

"Well, now she can take photographs of dolphins." Rourk smiled over at Keegan.

"I guess you better start working on your scuba license." Emerald sat back in her seat with the mug between her hands.

Keegan had thought for sure her mother would disapprove of her choice. But once again, she had surprised her. She hoped someday she would be as understanding of a mother.

"Oh, that's a great idea. Rourk, we should do that once we get to Washington. I've always wanted to scuba."

Richard and the boys walked through the door. Warrick came running up to his mother and held his arms up.

"What's this I hear about scuba? Did you already get picked up for a scuba team Rourk?" Richard took off his coat and tossed it over the chair. Emerald gave him a disapproving look so he picked it up and put it on the coat rack.

Keegan's dad was a big, burly man with flame-colored hair and a bushy beard. He looked dangerous because of all his visible scars, but in reality, he was just a teddy bear to those he loved. Keegan gave him a big smile.

"No, Keegan was just saying we should take classes together."

"That's a great idea. I'm quite certain you will

be picked up for a scuba team. They usually take the most physically fit. Never hurts to get a leg up."

"I'll find out soon what team I'm on."

Emerald moved to the stove and put on some more milk to make cocoa for the rest of them. Keegan loved being at home with her family.

Thaddeus sat down and filled them in on the day. They had been out teaching Warrick about tracking. He already knew the difference between a deer's print and a dog's—not too bad for a three-year-old. Richard grabbed a piece of paper and pencil off the counter and drew several different prints. He held it up to show Warrick. The baby walked over, staring at the paper silently for a moment.

"Deer." He pointed at the correct hoof.

"Dog." Warrick clapped.

"Bear?" Warrick asked.

Richard picked him up. "You got it. That's a bear. I think we have another warrior in the family, Emerald."

"I would hope so." She handed Warrick a marshmallow, and he struggled to get out of his father's arms. They all watched as he ran out of the room. It was amazing to see a young elf start to show signs of their powers.

"Emerald, did you tell them about their wedding gift yet?" Richard asked.

"No, I was waiting for you."

"We were trying to decide on a suitable gift, and your mother came up with a great idea. If you are interested, we'd like to give you the twenty acres around Keegan's spot. The place where you will be wed."

Keegan jumped up and ran around the table, throwing her arms around her father. "That's the best gift ever. Isn't it, Rourk?"

Rourk smiled. "Thank you. I agree, it's the perfect gift. We can build Keegan's dream house there."

Richard squeezed his daughter back. "Don't forget—I said it was your mother's idea."

Keegan reached over and hugged her mother. "I love you guys."

"Great. I thought we were rid of her." Thaddeus smirked.

"Oh hush, you will be out of the house by the time they move back. Take your brother into the play room." Emerald handed the youngest off to Thaddeus. Thaddeus mumbled under his breath but grabbed his brother and left. The little dog ran behind them.

Rourk opened the truck door for Keegan and the cold air hit her face. She pulled the plate of warm chocolate cookies closer to her body as they hurried up the walkway to Rourk's father's house.

Greg opened the door before they got there. "Come in. Get out of the cold."

Keegan handed him the plate of cookies. Greg peeked under the wrapping and grabbed a cookie. "Mmm, these are great. I have a soft spot for homemade cookies. Rourk's mother used to make them all the time."

"Rourk told me they were your favorite. Is that roast I smell? It smells delicious." Keegan shrugged off her coat and placed it on the coat hanger.

"Yes, it's pot roast. Rourk had to give me a

crash course in cooking before he left for the military. Whoever invented the crock-pot was a genius." Rourk's father led them into the living room. Rourk and Keegan sat on the couch while Greg took the seat across from them.

"So, this time next week, you will be my daughter-in-law. I wish Rourk's mother had been here to see it." Silence filled the room.

"I would love to have known her. I'm sure she was an amazing woman." Keegan looked over at Rourk. "My grandmother told me we would use the broom from your wedding."

Greg stood up. "That's right. I almost forgot about that tradition. I'll be right back." He hurried out of the room.

"Does it bother you to talk about your mother?" Keegan asked quietly.

Rourk shook his head. "It makes me miss her more, but I don't think that is a bad thing. I wish my father would talk about her more. I was so young when she died."

Greg walked in the room carrying a large box and set it down on the coffee table. He gingerly opened the wooden box; the hinge creaked. It obviously hadn't been opened in a while. Rourk and Keegan leaned forward in their seats to get a closer look.

Keegan's hand flew to her mouth. "Oh, thank you for sharing this with us."

Greg smiled sadly. "I've never been able to talk myself into opening this until now." He pulled out her long, off-white dress and brought it to his nose. "There's still the slight scent of lilacs. Your mother's favorite scent. That was the best day of my life."

He handed the dress to Keegan and pulled out a photo album. Rourk walked over and stood behind his father to look at the photographs. His parents made a striking couple: his father with his chiseled good looks and his mother with her natural beauty.

Keegan stood beside Rourk. "Your mother was breathtaking."

"That she was," Greg said softly. He shut the book and handed it to Rourk. "You two can look through the rest of this stuff. I need to check on dinner. This is harder than I expected." Moisture glistened in his eyes as he stood and walked to the kitchen.

Keegan placed her hand on Rourk's shoulder, not sure what to say.

"Why don't you look at what else is in there?" Rourk's voice sounded strained.

"Ok." Keegan knelt in front of the box and pulled out the most beautiful broom she had ever seen. It was handmade from dark brown twigs and wrapped in white ribbon that had shamrocks embroidered on it. Ivy climbed up the handle. Keegan ran her hands over the broom, her palms tingling, and she wondered how many generations it had been passed down. She closed her eyes and pictured Rourk's parents on their day and with smiles on their face as they jumped the broom.

"This is amazing." Keegan handed the broom to Rourk and looked back in the box. A green velvet box lay on the bottom. Keegan reached down and pulled the box out; she was curious to see what was inside.

She snapped the box open. A pair of blue sapphire and diamond antique earrings sparkled back at her.

Greg walked in the room and noticed the box. He gingerly took it from Keegan's hand, stared silently at them for a moment, and then handed the box back to Keegan. "These are yours. They were my mother's, and her mother's before that. I'm not sure how many daughters these have been passed down to. Hopefully, someday you will give me a granddaughter, and you can pass them on to her."

Keegan jumped up and threw her arms around Greg. "I'll be honored to wear them. Thank you."

Greg smiled. "You're welcome. Let's eat before it gets cold."

Rourk draped his arm over Keegan's shoulder as they walked to the dining room. She laid her head against him.

"Do you need any help?" Rourk asked.

"Sure. You can grab the drinks." Greg set the plate of roast in the center of the table, and went back for the rolls.

Keegan's stomach growled as Greg walked back into the room. He laughed. "Dig in! We don't want you wasting away on us."

She piled her plate with roast, potatoes, and vegetables. Rourk set a glass of water in front of her and then passed her a roll and the butter.

"Thank you." She smiled sweetly as she buttered the roll and took a bite.

"Dad, thanks for bringing out your wedding box to share with us. I know that wasn't easy for you," Rourk said quietly after some time had passed.

"It's what she would have wanted. Let's talk

about your wedding. Where are you going for your honeymoon?"

Keegan looked up sharply at Rourk. "He won't tell me. He says it's a surprise."

"Surprises are good. Did you have any trouble taking time off?" Greg asked.

"No, I was due for time off. With the holidays, it worked out well." Rourk could tell his father wanted to change the subject, so he went into details about his training and upcoming schedule. Keegan told him about switching schools and their new home.

After they ate, Rourk made coffee and they sat around the fireplace chatting. It was a nice evening, and Keegan was glad she got to know Rourk's father a little better. The rest of the weekend flew by and once again it was time to say goodbye.

They next time they would meet, it would be their wedding day.

Chapter 22

Keegan took a deep breath and tried to steady her nerves. Her heart was beating at such an accelerated pace she could feel it in her throat. She couldn't believe today was the day she had been waiting for since she was little girl.

The household had woken to the sound of pouring rain. In her pre-wedding panic attack, Keegan got hysterical over the weather, and her mother had to remind her that the weather manipulators in the family would take care of it.

"Besides," Emerald had said, brushing Keegan's hair behind her ears. She cupped her face in one hand. "Rain on your wedding day is good luck."

But the weather manipulators didn't need to do anything. Within an hour, the rain had let up and the sun was shining brightly.

Keegan really hoped she didn't trip or do something completely embarrassing. She was so nervous that she didn't know how she was going to make it to the ceremony spot. Thankfully, with elfin weddings she didn't have to walk there by herself. Rourk would be waiting downstairs for her and they would walk together. She loved that they stuck so close to their ancestors' traditions.

Her mother was expertly braiding white ribbon into a section of Keegan's auburn hair with her petite fingers. She glanced up in the mirror, catching her daughter's eye. "You look stunning."

Keegan flushed as there was a knock at the door.

"Is everyone decent?" Thaddeus called out.

"Yes," they said in unison.

Thaddeus walked through the door looking dashing in his military dress uniform. His hair had been slicked down so that it didn't stick up like usual, and his uniform was perfectly pressed. He looked like a young man instead of a boy, and it brought tears to Keegan's eyes.

"I can't believe you are making me dress up," Thaddeus complained. He had a small white box in his hands with a green bow tied around it.

"It's tradition." Emerald said simply.

Thaddeus walked across the room and offered Keegan the box. "Dad said I had to give this to you before you left. For luck."

Curious, Keegan reached for the box. She shook it—whatever was inside shifted with a thump. Tentatively, she unwrapped the bow and slowly lifted the lid. A huge grin spread across her full lips. She pulled out the horseshoe and stared at it. Her brother had obviously put a lot of time into it. It was painted green and had three shamrocks on each side with Keegan and Rourk written in calligraphy. "You did this?"

Thaddeus shrugged. "I came across it on one of my runs. I figured it was meant for you guys. Rourk could use all the luck he can get marrying you."

Keegan stood up, straightening her dress around her legs before she flung her arms around her brother. "I love it! Thank you so much. I can't wait to put it up in our house."

"Don't ever let it tip upside down or your luck will run out." Emerald's eyes twinkled. "You know you have to carry that with your bouquet."

"Really? Let me guess—tradition? Well, I will proudly carry it."

"Now, get out of here so Keegan can finish getting ready." Her mother shooed Thaddeus out the door.

Her mother pulled her hair into a loose bun, leaving a braid coiled on each side. She slipped some baby's breath in the back. Emerald grabbed the blush and swiped it across Keegan's cheekbones.

Keegan watched wide-eyed as her mother pulled the veil out of a box. It was beautiful—long and flowing with Celtic symbols embroidered on the bottom. She secured it on Keegan's bun and then pulled a layer over her face. "Perfect. Stand up so I can get some pictures. Remember don't remove the veil until the kiss."

Keegan set the horseshoe on her vanity table careful to make sure it didn't fall down. She stood up and stared at herself in the full-length mirror. She lightly touched Rourk's mother's earrings and hoped she was watching. Today, she would become Mrs. Kavanagh. She felt like a different person. She could feel the magic flowing through her veins. "Thank you, Mom."

"Give us a ten minute head start before you go downstairs to meet Rourk." Emerald cupped Keegan's cheeks and smiled, tears in her eyes. "I love you. You are simply radiant." Her mother hurried out of the room.

Keegan looked at the clock—ten minutes was going to feel like a lifetime. She sat on her chair and took deep, cleansing breaths. *You can do this.* Next thing she knew, she looked at the clock and exactly ten minutes had passed.

She stood up and slipped into her heels. She made it to the door before she realized her feet felt too constricted and kicked the shoes off. Barefoot felt right. Her hands shook as she reached for the doorknob. One last deep breath, and she pushed the door open.

Holding her dress at the sides so it wouldn't drag, she headed for the stairs, feeling like she was floating. She looked down the stairwell and met Rourk's eyes—the intensity of his stare was overpowering. She could feel his quiet confidence from where she stood, frozen to the spot. He looked so striking in his military uniform.

"You take my breath away. I've never seen a creature look more lovely," he said softly, holding out a hand for her.

Keegan slowly descended the stairs, clutching the flowers and the horseshoe. Each step brought her closer to her new life with her chosen. When she reached the final step, she grasped his hand and could have sworn sparks flew when their skin met.

"Are you ready?"

"Definitely." Keegan nodded her head and

laced her arm through her chosen's.

She wondered if Rourk could hear her heart pounding. It seemed to vibrate in her ears.

They stepped outside and the warmth of the sun greeted them. Birds were chirping all around, and there wasn't a single cloud in the sky. It wasn't cold, but just right—she knew that was a gift from the weather manipulators. Celtic music could be heard in the distance. Keegan squeezed Rourk's arm, and he smiled down at her.

Once they reached the clearing, Keegan inhaled sharply. She felt like she was in a fairy-tale. How had they managed to pull this together in such a short amount of time? Magic, of course. She smiled to herself. Her special oasis had turned into a botanical garden. Brightly colored flowers and lush greens replaced the bare winter grounds. Rows of white chairs flanked the spot where they would be wed; each chair was hung with purple lilacs.

As they approached, the Wedding March flowed through the air and everyone turned in their seats. Rows and rows of elfin families smiled back at them. Her heart felt full with love.

Anna gave her a small wave, and Lauren grinned. Thaddeus and Tommy were standing to the left and the girls to the right. The priestess, Sarah, stood in the middle with the cords draped on her arm. She had married Keegan's parents and most of the elves there.

Keegan felt like everything was moving in slow motion. She could feel the magic flowing through the air and the joy radiating off everyone around them. It smelled like a beautiful spring day with flowers in bloom. The stream trickled soothingly. Keegan tried to take it all in, to save the memory.

Sarah smiled warmly when they reached her. She was a lovely woman with a tall, willowy body and clear, pale skin. Her face was long, her eyes clear green, and her hair was crisp white and in a braid down the side of her chest. She cleared her throat.

"Today, Rourk and Keegan will be joined in a handfasting. Their hands will be tied together with a knot that binds them in such a way that they choose to be bound. This ritual symbolizes their oneness not only with each other but with all creation and thus their union is blessed, it's sacredness recognized by all creation.

"The soul shares characteristics with all things divine. It is this belief which assigned virtues to the cardinal directions: East, South, West and North. It is in this tradition that a blessing is offered in support of this ceremony." She paused.

Keegan felt the crowd behind them hold their breath

Raising both hands to the air, Sarah went on. "Blessed be this union with the gifts of the East. Communication of the heart, mind, and body. Fresh beginnings with the rising of each sun. The knowledge of the growth found in the sharing of silences.

"Blessed be this union with the gifts of the South. Warmth of hearth and home. The heat of the heart's passion. The light created by both for the lightest, the darkest of times.

"Blessed be this union with the gifts of the West. The deep commitments of the lake. The swift excitement of the river. The refreshing cleansing of the rain. The all encompassing passion of the sea.

"Blessed be this union with the gifts of the North. Firm foundation on which to build. Fertility of the fields to enrich your lives. A stable home to which you may always return."

Sarah smiled on Keegan and Rourk as she lowered her arms. "Each of these blessings from the four cardinal directions emphasizes those things which will help you build a happy and successful union. Yet, they are only tools. Tools which you must use together to create what you seek in this union.

"Know that before you go further, since your spirits have crossed in this life, you have formed ties between each other. As you seek to enter into this state of matrimony, you should strive to make real the ideals which give meaning to both this ceremony and the institution of marriage.

"With full awareness, know that you are declaring your intent to be handfasted before your friends and family, present, absent, and departed. The promises made today, and the ties that are bound here, will greatly strengthen your union; they will cross the years and lives of each soul's growth."

Smiling, Sarah asked them, "Do you still seek to enter into this ceremony?

Together, Rourk and Keegan spoke. "We do."

"Rourk and Keegan, I bid you look into each other's eyes." Sarah waited while they turned their eyes to one another, and then went on. "Will you honor and respect one another, and seek to never break that honor?"

Keegan smiled at Rourk as they answered, "We will."

Sarah draped the blue cord over their hands.

"And so the first binding is made," she said. "Will you share each other's pain and seek to ease it?"

"We will."

She wrapped the yellow cord around them. "And so the binding is made. Will you share the burdens of each so that your spirits may grow in this union?"

"We will."

Sarah draped the white cord and smiled. "And so the binding is made. Will you share each other's laughter, and look for the brightness in life and the positive in each other?"

"We will."

She draped the red cord around their hands. "And so the binding is made." She swiftly tied the cords into three knots. "Rourk and Keegan, as your hands are bound together now, so your lives and spirits are joined in a union of love and trust. The knots of this binding are not formed by these cords but, rather, by the vows you have made. For always, you hold in your own hands the fate of this union. Above you are the stars and below you is the earth. Like the stars, your love should be a constant source of light, and like the earth, a firm foundation from which to grow. Have patience with one another. For storms will come, but they will go quickly. Be free in the giving of affection and warmth.

Sarah produced the two wedding rings, holding out her palm where they sparkled in the sunlight. "A circle is the symbol of the sun and the earth and the universe. It is a symbol of holiness and of perfection and of peace. In these rings, it is the symbol of unity, in which your lives are now joined in one unbroken circle, in which, wherever you go, you will always return to your shared life together.

"As you have stated your desire to be united, one with the other, take now these rings and place them upon each other's finger, as pledge and testimony to your love and commitment to each other."

Rourk reached forward and his hand shook slightly as he placed the braided white-gold ring on Keegan's finger. A magical hum raced through her body.

Keegan smiled and placed a larger version of the ring on Rourk's finger.

"I now proclaim you are husband and wife, thus are your hands fasted, two are now made one." Sarah opened her hands and grinned. "You may seal your union to your chosen with a kiss."

Rourk gathered the veil in his hands and pushed it over Keegan's head so that it fell down her back. He leaned forward, lightly pressed his lips to hers, and then intensified the kiss. Keegan got lost in the kiss, forgetting her surroundings. When Rourk finally pulled away, loud cheers went up from the crowd.

"Settle down. It's not over yet." Sarah laughed. She looked back to Rourk and Keegan. "This will be your first act of working together as a couple.

"Brooms are used for cleaning and sweeping. Therefore, that they are used to symbolize the sweeping away the remnants of the past which no longer serve us is appropriate. The sword symbolizes the wielding of power and personal responsibility. As the bride and groom jump they are reminded that remaining vigilant over these aspects of the day to day shall help them to achieve the quality of life that they aspire to. Anna, Lauren, and Thaddeus—will you now lay down the Sword and Broom?"

Anna and Lauren walked forward and laid down the broom.

Thaddeus came forward and crossed the broom with the sword.

"Now putting the past behind you, and remembering that you have the power to create a strong future. Jump together into your new lives."

Keegan grabbed Rourk's hand and gave him a reckless smile. He shook his head, smiling in return. Together, they jumped and landed safely on the other side. Keegan laughed and Rourk pulled her in for another kiss. As they broke apart, Keegan looked up at her guests and was surprised to see two tigers in the distance. One was obviously Donald—she would have known his form anywhere. And by his side was the white tiger.

Relief filled Keegan, and she was content knowing Donald was going to be alright. As usual, her brother was right.

Bagpipes began to play. Rourk wrapped his arms around Keegan, swinging her around and around. As other guests stood to join in, Keegan felt on top of the world.

"Are you ready?" Rourk asked with a smile on his handsomely rugged face.

Keegan nodded and grasped his warm hand in hers. With the other, she reached for the teleporter's hand. Keegan closed her eyes as her stomach dropped.

A moment later, Rourk squeezed her hand. "Open your eyes."

Keegan did and found she was staring up at a huge castle. She dropped Rourk's hand, rushing forward to grip the stone wall that surrounded it. The lawns around it stretched emerald green, while the mountains cradled it on three sides. It was gray stone and several stories high with more turrets than she could count. From a flag pole near the long drive, an orange, white, and green flag waved.

Her eyes danced with excitement as she turned and clapped her hands, her eyes on her husband. "Ireland?"

"Of course. Where else would I take you?"

Rourk turned to the elf that had transported them. "Thanks, Pete."

The silent man nodded and disappeared.

Keegan took a deep breath. "So. This is it. Are you nervous?"

Rourk's eyes met hers and he smiled deviously. "I can't wait. Let's get inside."

Keegan looked at the ground. "We don't have any bags?"

"Already in the room." He took her hand, and they hurried up the massive stone steps.

As Rourk reached for the large black handle, Keegan ran her hand down the intricately carved designs in the wooden door.

"It's beautiful," she whispered.

Rourk agreed and pushed on the door.

It opened to a large lobby, warmly lit by huge, iron chandeliers. The stone floors were covered in elegant Persian rugs and littered with antique furniture. They walked to the counter against the right wall.

A plump woman with red hair piled loosely in a bun on top of her head broke into a warm smile. "Dia dui."

"Dia is Muire duit," Rourk replied. "Reservation is under Kavanagh."

She glanced down at her ledger. "Ah yes, the newlyweds. I won't keep you. Here's your keys, room 303." She winked at Keegan as she handed the keys to Rourk.

Keegan felt her face flush.

They took the stairs to their room, stealing glances at each other and laughing. Once they got to the third floor, Rourk stopped and abruptly turned towards Keegan. Her heart skipped a beat when she looked up into his grey eyes.

He gently traced the side of her face causing her whole body to tingle. "Keegan, I am honored to be your chosen. I will spend the rest of my life trying to be the best husband possible."

"I hope someday I am worthy of your love—." Her words were cut off as his lips met hers, and he scooped her up in his arms.

Keegan laughed as he carried her through the door and down the hall to their room. She barely noticed the beauty of the hotel—the wooden walls and the pretty carpeted floors, all illuminated by lights shaped like torches on the walls. Her eyes were strictly for Rourk.

He fumbled with the key and pushed the door to their room open, then slowly lowered her to the ground. She glanced around at the beautiful room, and her eyes stopped at the huge wooden bed waiting for them.

Rourk came up behind her. He pressed his lips to her neck as he unzipped her dress. It fell to the floor, and shivers ran down her spine. She had been waiting for this moment for a long time. Slowly, she turned to face him.

"You're incredible." His voice sounded rougher than usual.

Keegan's hands shook as she tried to unbutton his shirt. His body felt so warm under her touch. She ran her hands up his muscular chest and sighed, her heart pounding. All of her senses were heightened, and her skin was on fire.

Rourk gently led her to the bed.

Hours later, she rolled to her side and rested her head in her hand, staring at Rourk. "Wow," was all she could manage to say.

He was resting against his pillow, both of his hands behind his head. There was still the faint glistening of sweat on his beautiful chest. Rourk grinned. "Well worth the wait."

"You can say that again." Keegan scooted closer and laid her head on his chest. His heart beat steadily beneath her ear. "I'm so excited to spend the rest of my life with you."

Rourk's arms wrapped around her again, pulling her close beneath the covers. In the dim light of the room, Keegan closed her eyes and fell asleep to the sound of her husband's heartbeat.

Acknowledgments

I would like to thank Claire Teeter and Heather Adkins, my editors. They have both helped me grow as a writer. My children for their understanding. My husband for his encouragement. My youngest sister, Katrina, for being my biggest fan. Eden Crane Designs for the beautiful cover. Mostly, I would like to thank my readers who make this all worthwhile. Thank you!

About the Author

Julia Crane is the author of the <u>Keegan's Chronicles</u> series. She has a bachelor's degree in criminal justice. Julia has believed in magical creatures since the day her grandmother first told her an Irish tale. Growing up her mother greatly encouraged reading and using your imagination. Although she's spent most of her life on the US east coast, she currently lives in Dubai with her husband and three children.

Find Julia online at juliacraneauthor.com